Guthrie's Lot Part 2

A Level Path

Olwyn Harris

Reading Stones Publishing

Published by: Reading Stones Publishing
              Helen Brown & Wendy Wood
Cover Design: Wendy Wood

For more copies contact the publisher at:

Glenburnie Homestead
212 Glenburnie Road
ROB ROY NSW 2360
Mobile: 0422 577 663
Email: hbrown19561@gmail.com

For Helen, my mentor, who gave
confidence to my steps and direction to
what was inside. Thank you for being part
of this journey!

A Level Path

They will come with weeping;
they will pray as I bring them back.
I will lead them beside streams of water
on a level path
where they will not stumble...
(Jeremiah 31:9)

Olwyn Harris

1968

1.

Iris held her passport and stepped forward slowly in line. Her sleepless eyes stared in a glazed stupor at the tasselled beads on the shirt in front of her. She felt so tired she couldn't even revel in this moment, but she was here. That was a miracle in itself. She half smiled and half felt like crying as she thought about how her Mum would break the news to her father. She handed over her passport and answered his questions by rote: "Iris Camilla Guthrie". He stamped and handed it back to her. "Enjoy your stay in the Old Country, Miss."

She just wanted to sleep. She had booked a room at a kind of hostel arrangement: central and... clean. The brochure mentioned a couple of times that Whitedale Lodge was clean. It was obviously something they believed was a selling point. Iris started trailing through her map of the subway when a man in flared pants and a skin-tight beige shirt sidled up to her. "Hey Sweet-sugar, need a hand?" She grinned at his proper sounding accent. It just didn't go with the greasy swagger of his hips, his big hair and huge ego. He seemed to think her smile was an invitation and he moved in; way too close.

"Pretty right, thanks," she said with a sudden frown and turned away, clutching her handbag.

"Oooh. A little Aussie mate – hey? Cool. Don't get you lost now. I can show where to go Sweet-sugar."

"Oh, my goodness. If I wanted help I would ask!" When he didn't go away, she stared at him in disgust. "You have got to be kidding me! Leave me alone!" When he didn't move, she said quietly and firmly, "Leave now or I start screaming."

He laughed, lit up a cigarette and shrugged. "Right you are then Sweet-sugar..." and he sauntered off. She watched his big hair, moving in to chat up another lost looking traveller. She shivered. What a creep! Iris quickly looked around for someone in uniform, someone official, someone reliable.

She found a lady in an orange miniskirt and jacket looking very proper and asked directions. It wasn't far. She was given a sketchy brochure and she followed it to the subway; she sat down on her suitcase and sighed while she waited. Soon. Bed. Soon. Her brain was fuzzy and navigating all the busyness of this strange place seemed to take so much longer than she would have believed possible. She felt a little bit overwhelmed, and a big bit frightened by the sheer quantity of people. This was so different to Gumleigh. It seemed like she had landed on another planet.

She listened to the announcements, but the noise and the accent made it hard to understand. She checked the timetable to Paddington. Yes, this was her. She boarded, dragging her luggage, listening with focused attention to every station stop. She then had to change lines for the station nearest to Whitedale. "Take the six-twenty.... Platform two," that's what the attendant said. New ticket. New train. She got her ticket, she sat on the bench and felt like throwing up. She was so tired. Everything felt weird and distorted. She wondered if she was in a 'Doctor Who" episode. Perhaps they didn't allow sleep in this country, and it was an alien plot to send people mad or to capture them as extra-terrestrial slaves. She struggled with her bag when the train pulled up. Before she could even sit down it lurched forward, hurtling her handbag out of her grasp, spewing everything all over the floor. She scrambled to pick up her things. How soon until she would get to the Lodge? And bed... the sway of the train was rhythmic, numbing. The rumble of the tracks lulled her senses. Even the hard vinyl seats seemed comfortable. How was it possible that she could relax here, and not sleep a moment on the plane when she had hours and hours to kill?

The announcer muffled a distorted station-name. Had she dozed off? "Here already..." she murmured. The attendant had been right. It wasn't far. She was relieved, but she'd check at the ticket-booth to be sure. She didn't really understand anything anyone said. They all spoke so quickly in their thick accents.

Well, as it happened, clarifying anything with the bored, gum-chewing Miss-with-attitude and long eyelashes in the booth, would be like asking a block of wood to speak words. She repeated herself... again. And she got the same garbled response. A lady nearby heard her question and sympathetically gave her a smile. "We just came from Whitedale yesterday."

Iris smiled. "Is it nice? The brochure said it was clean..."

"Oh it's pristine! You'll love it. You need to take the bus from here though..." and she gave her a glorious smile that covered her thick cockney accent, and reassuringly led Iris down the stairs and pointed her in the right direction.

Iris was torn between being grateful and just plain mad. The travel agent in Blackstone had been so animated when she secured the reservation: the central location would be such a convenient base. This was not convenient. It was costing her a fortune in public transport. And time. Time she could be sleeping. She might give that feedback when she gets back, to protect some other poor traveller from this torture. Sleep deprivation was a well-established technique for breaking the hardest resistance. Iris admitted it. She was broken. If she hadn't already paid for the booking, she would have just let it go and found somewhere closer. But her budget was tight… so she needed to keep as many prepaid arrangements as possible. She climbed onto the bus and sat down. She wanted to stay awake and absorb all these first sights and sounds of London bathed in glorious morning light, but the muted buzz of a transistor radio held in the hand of the passenger in front of her, and the mumble of the bus engine underneath her, and the vibration beside her as she leant against the window, lulled her into a hypnotic sleep.

Within moments someone was shaking her awake. "Miss? Are you getting off here?" She struggled to her feet and the driver pulled out her luggage from the stowage. Iris smiled her thanks and asked directions to Whitedale Lodge.

"You mean that little English pub just there?" He pointed to the inn across the cobbled street. "It's traditional. Lots of atmosphere. You'll enjoy that. The young ones always do."

"Doesn't *'atmosphere'* mean noise? Oh no. I want sleep. The brochure said the Lodge was clean... central... and quiet. I *really* need quiet. I have got to sleep!"

"Well, that place is definitely more a pumping pub than quiet Lodge. Sure will be noisy if you're needing to sleep off the jet-lag. Although there's that little backpacker place out on Faulkner's Farm. That might be quieter. It is peak season though. This is a bit of a migratory roosting place, but they might have space. Not many options in Brightdale unfortunately."

"Brightdale?" She looked uneasily across the little cobbled streets of the small English village. The sign at the bus stop was faded but there was no doubt it said Brightdale. "Oh no. No! *White*dale. Not Brightdale! I asked for directions to Whitedale Lodge."

He smiled sympathetically. "Hmm. Well I'm guessing they told you how to get to Brightdale. Seems you followed your directions jolly well, because you are definitely here at Brightdale." He chuckled. "Welcome to Brightdale." He winked at her good naturedly. "I used to have an aunt live here. It's not a bad sort of place. Overall, it will probably meet your condition for quiet."

Iris rummaged in her handbag for a sheet of paper and pushed it to him. "But how do I get to there? I have paid for my accommodation for tonight. I need to get there." She sat down on her bag as another wave of nausea hit her. She took a deep breath... and then other.

He looked at the sheet and then looked at Iris. He cleared his throat. "Do you know where you are?"

"Brightdale... evidently," she said. She took a deep shuddering breath, and everything within her tried not to cry.

"Hmm. What I be meaning is... that the bus back to London is only a daily service... a full four-hour trip. You look dead-beat. If I was you, I'd be looking for a room. It's a nice little place this. You might want to stay and have a look around since your here.

"At this stage, I don't want to look at anything. I just want sleep! I could take the park-bench. I'm exhausted."

"Loitering would have a Bobby move you on, or take you in. That would solve your accommodation problem though," he said with a grin. "Like I was sayin', the pub is noisy sort of affair. So I'd be suggesting you go for the local Backpacker Lodge. Faulkner's Road is off the main road... quieter than the pub."

"Yeah, probably not the pub. Where's Faulkner's Road?"

"Do you want a cab?"

"I've already spent my money on tonight's accommodation, and now I have to do it again. I'm going to have to walk."

He shrugged. He didn't think she'd make it. Pulled out his map and scanned the page, rotating it once. He pointed down the street to the intersection. "Take this road, turn right onto Grosvenor Street. That'd be at the phone booth there... then right onto Pike... then Faulkner is on your left. The backpacker Lodge is along there a bit, on the right. Sure you don't want a lift?"

"Right – Grosvenor; right – Pike; Faulkner – left. Got it. I'll be fine."

"Hey... look Love, get back on and I'll detour. Got to turn around to get back on the motorway anyway," he said compassionately as he climbed back in the bus.

Iris nodded and swiped her eyes. "Thank you," she whispered gratefully. She was pretty sure she could not have walked all that way lugging her suitcase.

"Good luck to you then," he said when he pulled up at the gate. He sounded like he was offering last rites as he wound open the door for her to get off.

Everything would be okay if she could just sleep. She had never been so obsessed with the idea before. But then, she could never remember a time when her bed wasn't made, pillows plumped, and sheets folded at the corners; always available. That sounded so wonderful just now.

Iris picked up her bag and stepped down off the bus. She had no idea exactly when she got off track. It's not like she had a problem asking for directions. If people just slowed down when they spoke, she'd get a handle on their accent. But right now, she was standing in the driveway of Faulkner Farmstay Lodge wondering how she ended up here.

≁⊱⊰≀

2.

It looked sort of quaint. A rusted metal sign swung near the gate in the breeze, squeaking out a welcome in a homely unpretentious sort of way. The woman frowned and said they were full. Iris didn't have a reservation, which was essential at this time of year. Iris begged and pulled out a wad of pound notes. The woman shrugged and then nodded reluctantly. Iris trailed behind the landlady's angular frame and bent legs, dragging her bag up the narrow stairs. "You'll have to stay in the main house since our regular rooms are all full. Given you are only staying the one night we can make do. Peak season," she muttered.

Iris didn't notice the tasteless floral wallpaper or the strong smell of lavender, or the overlaying stale sort of mustiness of the carpet. She was barely able to stay awake as she sat in the tiny awkward bathroom. All she saw was that the pillowcase was clean. Clean. *The proprietors of Whitedale would be proud*, she thought as her head hit the printed linen. She went out like a light.

When she roused, Iris could barely open her eyes. She lay on the bed, trying to work out where she was. What day was it? What did she have to do today? Everything felt strange... very strange. She opened her eyelids slowly and groggily looked around the room;

everything was blurry and unclear. It took her a while to remember. Plane, train, bus... Where was she? England. England? She was in England! She lay there absorbing that thought. There was a dark old-fashioned timber wardrobe and a miss-match of bedroom furniture, but not in a good way. There were bright garish throws and cushions, mixed with pallid floral wallpaper, pastel paint and purple printed linen. The attempt to modernise the room created a combination that looked a lot like a Turkish bizarre. She tried to retrace her steps on how she got here, but it was shrouded in a fuzzy haze of airports and train-stations and bus terminals and multiple faces giving her directions. She dozed off again.

Iris stirred to the sounds of yelling and some unreserved clanging pots. She could not hear what the argument was about, but it was certainly not quiet. Hmm. Perhaps the pub would have been a better option after all. She covered her head with a pillow, but it did little to muffle the raucous commotion. She groaned. Didn't seem like she was going back to sleep now. The shouting punctuated with clanking kitchenware made certain she was well and truly awake. Slowly, she sat up and got out of bed; lifted the blind and peered out the little casement window. The sun was setting low on the horizon. Huh. She groaned and thought she would have slept longer. Still after some dinner, she might go back to sleep again.

Another night's sleep and then she was sure she would be ready to start her English adventure, full throttle, first thing in the morning.

Iris went into the bathroom and slowly attended to her ablutions. Her head was layered in cotton wool; it was hard to focus. She found it hard to work the plumbing in the shower and ended up allowing a rather cold dribble trickle over her back as she tried to wash off the multiple layers of travel stains. She cleaned her teeth, but overall, she didn't felt much better. She pulled on her jeans and shirt, becoming intrigued that the energy of the argument downstairs had hardly abated. She peered into the little framed mirror and tried to tidy her hair. The landlady should be able to give her a copy of the bus timetable back to London. Her holiday plan included going around quality restaurants, shopping on Carnaby Street and lots of galleries. That's what she wanted: to experience London – shops, theatre, art, music, culture. If she fancied doing country – she could have stayed home. She did country every day there. Her plan was that this trip would be different. Very different.

By the time Iris made her way down the steep, narrow stairway, the uproar had subsided into an eerie sort of vacant stillness. She ducked under the low overhang of the staircase and stood in the entryway for a moment. Huh. Silence. Then Iris made her way through the corridor looking for the owner, calling as she went, "Hello?"

She looked around the kitchen. The old wooden benches were marked and dinted from years of scrubbing and cutting. Iris knew kitchens and for an old-fashioned country farmhouse kitchen, this one was well appointed. Someone had gone to a lot of effort to update it; to accommodate the requirements of catering and retain its old-world charm. There were brass-bottomed pots and cast-iron pans hanging along a rack suspended from the ceiling, and the deep double-sink was clogged full of pots that may have well been used as the percussion in the argument. There was a knife-block, and several modern appliances sitting on the bench. She went over to the gas stove and dubiously looked in a large pot sitting there. Its contents were burping like a miniature lake of molten mud. It seemed strange that no one was around. Iris looked around, and called out again, introducing herself. Silence. She tentatively picked up the wooden spoon and gave the gloop a stir and turned off the heat. It had burnt on the bottom of the pot. She checked the oven and the smell of cake filled the room. It was stodgy in the middle and charred around the edges. She took it out and let it sit a few minutes before turning it onto a rack to cool. She looked around some more and checked some drawers curiously.

She found a spoon and tested the stew on the stove and spat it out into the sink. That was disgusting! She quickly poured herself a glass a water and gulped, trying to rid her palate of the filthy taste. Glue stew and burnt cake? Surely this was not dinner? She would not be eating – that's for sure. She scanned the bench for a recipe but couldn't find one. She had a look in the cupboards, for some herbs, or condiments, or veges, but every shelf seemed bare of the essential culinary basics. Just then she spotted another door around the corner and opened it. She stood amazed as she looked in at the most incredible farmhouse walk-in pantry. Many of the shelves had large sections of bare space but here at least were some options. Mainly tinned ones. Fresh produce seemed like an unknown phenomenon here.

She stepped forward and considered how the stew might be salvaged when someone behind her cleared his throat, "Ahem."

Iris jumped and spun around blushing brightly. "Oh. Hi. I'm Iris. I'm staying in a room here."

"Ahh. Rip van Winkle? From Australia. You're awake! Welcome to Faulkner's Farmstay."

"I did sleep... but not well, thanks to the disturbance involving the clanging of a lot of pots and pans. I would say Rip van Winkle was ripped off some well-deserved sleep... my twenty years of allocated rest were cut short."

"Ahh! Your short-changed slumber had my Mother so concerned yesterday that she wanted to check you were still breathing. I told her to let you be. If you died, the smell would clue us in." There was a cheeky twinkle in his eye that appealed to her.

"I doubt that could have happened. The stench from whatever concoction this is, dominates all other smells." Iris tilted her head and frowned into the pot. Then she turned and stared at the man leaning on the kitchen bench. "Did you say yesterday? Today is Wednesday, right?"

He shook his head. "Thursday. All day: morning – noon – to dusk.

"Thursday? Have I really been asleep for a day and a half?"

He raised his brow and nodded. "Yep. Rip van Winkle."

Iris closed her eyes and rubbed the line of her eyebrows. "Well, the hospitality here is heart-warming to say the least: there was a commotion that could wake the dead; the place is deserted; and your guests are left to rot."

"Deserted. Oh yes. Sorry about that. There's been a bit of an emergency. Vino, our cook, up and left. He was from Naples. I made the mistake of giving him rather specific feedback from the guesthouse. He had a very "Italian" melt-down. No amount of talking would salve his wounded pride. Not that he could cook anyway. I thought the term was a little generous when applied to what he served up."

"Ahh. So it was Vino who woke me with his enthusiastic pot-clanging? Is this his?" she tilted her chin towards the burping sludge.

He shrugged and nodded apologetically.

"Then perhaps the feedback wasn't a mistake. Do you think it is a bad thing he left?"

He looked at her suspiciously. "You wouldn't know your way around a kitchen, would you Iris? We've had the place renovated... but that's really of no benefit if there isn't anyone who can use it. Mother asked me to hold the fort, to keep dinner on the boil while she has gone into the village to try and find someone to fill in."

Iris grinned as she looked at this disarmingly charming young man. Outdoorsy type. He had on a college sweatshirt. He definitely would prefer to be out playing cricket in his whites, or in a rowing team. Anything but a kitchen. Even the farm setting didn't seem like him. "She might come back with someone..." Iris suggested hopefully.

He shrugged. "Maybe. Except that we took the guy from Naples in the first place because none of the locals were interested."

"No one?"

He shook his head dramatically. "No one can cook here."

"How is that possible? Everyone knows how to cook. It's like learning to breathe, or walk, or read..."

"Perhaps Brightdale is occupied by illiterate cripples who need respirators..." he said with a grin. "But still no cooks."

Iris laughed. "You're not very kind to your own."

"Just honest. I'm on semester break. This Lodge is the dream of my parents. But Father died three years back and..."

"Oh, I'm sorry..."

He looked at the sympathy that filled her eyes. "This has been Mother's life. Kept her going no doubt, but the reality of it is harder than the dreaming sometimes. She doesn't cook either."

"Oh. Well, I am aware that I only paid for one night. It seems I owe you extra..." She said it to see if would pick up on her plight... and her implied offer for a solution.

"How about... you cook dinner for our guests, and we work out something for the accommodation." He went over to a drawer and handed her an apron.

"Full exchange? I owe you nothing," said Iris.

"I'll owe you, if you do this for me."

"Okay... done. How many guests?"

"Fourteen. We've converted the stables – six rooms downstairs and six in the loft. A couple are twin-share. Just now we are full."

"Oh, that's all? And your family... anyone else?" Fishing.

"Only mother and me." He grinned.

"So. Sixteen. Me... seventeen. Well, that shouldn't be too hard. Do you have meat?"

"I think there is Lamb. That's all Vino used." He dug in the yellow box freezer and prized free a couple of lumps of mince.

Iris looked at the clock. "When do you normally serve dinner?"

"In half an hour..."

"Oh. Well, you can have what's in that pot for wallpapering. I'll start fresh."

"You recognise glue when you see it. This is an encouraging start."

Iris laughed. "It won't be flash... and..." She glanced at the clock; "It will be a few minutes late. If you could apologise to your guests and tell them I'll be serving dinner at seven this evening." She took the scarf from her neck and wrapped it around her head, so her fringe was held up out of the way and washed her hands.

"Do you need a hand?" he asked stepping back out of her way as she took command.

Iris shook her head.

"Oh, I'm Stanbury Atworth by the way. Call me Stan."

"Hi Stan," she said with a smile, "I'm Iris Guthrie. One impromptu farmhouse dinner coming up."

He shook his head in admiration. "That sounds amazing. I'll go and tell Mother the good news."

She came out of the pantry with her arms full of tins of tomatoes and mushrooms and asparagus and other bits and pieces. "Just hold the review until you taste it. You might have to give me feedback from your house-guests too." The cook from Naples obviously felt familiar with pasta, so pasta it would be. She piled it all on the bench and took the glue outside and dumped it in a dilapidated garden near the back fence. Even the weeds wilted under it. Iris gagged and grimaced as she went back inside. Unbelievable.

She couldn't find any veges, except for a couple of potatoes with long stringing shoots sprouting from their eyes, a wilted onion, a few shrivelled apples and a string of garlic hanging from the window. Well. That was a start. She felt optimistic that if the guests were familiar with glue as a staple, it had the potential to make even a basic fare look grand. She scraped the bottom of the pot with a spatula, soaked it, and grabbed a fresh one from the hooked rack hanging from the rafters. The water was on a boil in no time at all. She put the lump of mince on the stove to thaw. She used another saucepan to sauté the sad little onion, garlic, potatoes. It was hard for her to contemplate cooking without fresh produce. Really? Didn't they know about garden fresh tomatoes? Or herbs? It felt fraudulent to be cooking without it and authenticity in the kitchen was important to her. That was the heritage of her grandfather's garden. He was always bringing over fresh produce by the basket full.

Iris found her rhythm, moving back and forth like a dance. Then she opened can, after can, after can, tipping the contents into the pot, stirring with the wooden spoon. She was humming a tune, searching for the condiments and put them out on the wooden table. She looked up and stopped still. Stanbury was standing at the door, entranced by the picture before him. She blushed and smiled. "Is everything to your satisfaction Mister?" she asked with a playful bow.

"Oh, I believe my satisfaction levels just went up in leaps and bounds. I've told everyone that Vino has left, and dinner will be worth their attendance this evening. Although, you do have your work cut out for you... they are a sceptical lot."

She shrugged. "Do you, by any chance, have fresh herbs in your garden... some Basil or Oregano perhaps?"

Stanbury shrugged. "Could be. My father was a fair gardener, but like I said, no one's done anything with it since. Gardening, along with cooking, has not been on Mother's list of preferred hobbies. It was never my thing, either."

Iris stopped. "Oh. No problem. I just didn't see many herbs in the pantry."

"I'll see what I can find..." He went out the door and returned with a wilted twig of rather sad looking yellowed oregano. "Hmm. It's a bit sad."

Iris pounced on it. "I'm desperate. It'll do. Consider it sun-dried." A little bit of frantic chopping, stirring, draining, serving. "Nearly done. You can call your guests."

Stan went out and rang the traditional European cow-bell hanging by the courtyard door, and the guests appeared, lining up with plates.

When they had cleared and washed up, Iris sat at the kitchen table with a teapot. "Thanks for your help Stan. I think we did well," she said with a grin as she took a sip from her cup.

He sat down with a furrowed frown and poured himself a cup of tea. "I did get some very specific feedback from the guests," he said. He sat drinking a cup of tea soberly.

Iris stared at him shocked. It never occurred to her that her offerings would secure the same protests as Vino-from-Naples. Perhaps these guests were not just sceptical... but held impossible gourmet expectations. Surely, they were not going to complain when she was just doing them a favour! It was very possible the next cook would hear about the little Australian cook – Iris from Gumleigh, who had an Aussie tantrum and stormed out leaving them in the lurch because she couldn't take feedback. She took a deep breath and tried to settle herself from freaking out.

Stanbury pursed his lips and nodded soberly. "They were deadly serious. They said that if I let you go; they would all pack up and leave with you." Then he laughed. "Just kidding! You look like I was lining you up in front of a firing squad. How could you even think it wasn't perfect? They all said the meal they had tonight was the best they've had! That's high praise with all their travelling around."

Iris blinked and felt her shoulders relax. "They liked it? It was just a basic Neapolitan, which was a bit of a risk, given that your Vino was from Naples."

"Nothing little Vino offered remotely compares to anything with the reputation of Naples. And we had desert. Two courses! The apple layer cake (with custard!) got great reviews: "good, homely, farmhouse fare" – that is what they said they loved. You out-did anything we've had here on every level, and without any lead-time! But all this does leave me with a huge problem. We need our guests to stay and pay. Mother can't afford a mass exodus just now. We have to make the most of the season for as long as we can. The idea of including food was meant to be an incentive: travelling on a budget without having to worry about meals... if it is edible of course. Vino insulted the concept. But you... you just bought us a great deal of credibility. I want you to stay on to the close of the season."

Iris smiled at his eager expression. It bordered on desperate. "I'm flattered. Truly. But I'm here on a holiday. My plan to do a food tour was not about cooking it. And I have theatre, and sight-seeing, and galleries and shopping on my list." She held up her hand. "That wasn't grocery shopping by the way. I didn't come to England to cook in a country-house kitchen. I do that at home."

"Please. What do I need to do to convince you? We'll pay you of course."

Iris would not be moved. "Thanks, but no thanks."

"But..."

"The only '*but*' here is my holiday." She had taken this holiday out of her savings, so Dad couldn't say... Never mind, the budget was tight to be sure, but it wasn't impossible, and she wasn't about to give it up, even to help nice people out in a jam.

He considered her face, determined and smiling. There was no possible way he was letting this woman walk out of his life just like that. "What if... what if you cook during the week, and then on the weekends I give you any tour you like? We could do it together. I know London like the back of my hand. You know, make it a long weekend... every weekend. I've heard Aussies say it is the land of the long weekend. You can have Friday off as well: Monday through to Thursday. That's fair. It will mean you have accommodation... we have a designated room in the Lodge for the cook. The quarters have been upgraded... the conversion of the stables was finished last season. Very modern. You'll have the days to yourself – we only offer breakfast and evening dinners. This way you get to have your holiday... and a little extra cash. We both win. Come on. Let's just try it for a while. See how it goes."

⚜

3.

After breakfast was cleaned up – porridge pots scrubbed and pans washed, Iris had a look over the pantry in more detail, and gave it a more logical order. She went through the cupboards, working out where things were. She couldn't serve pasta every night, so she chose the menu to use what was in stock, and made up a shopping list to fill in the gaps.

Then Mrs Atworth called a meeting. The woman sat there stiffly, her chin jutting out and her shoulders scrunched. Iris was sure the woman had made up her mind that anything Iris could offer would be just another version of Vino's insulting cooking from Naples. Iris had been so sure Stan had been speaking credibly, that she hadn't even thought it necessary to go over the details of the arrangement. However, that smouldering look of disgust on his mother's face made it blatantly clear to Iris that Mrs Atworth resented her presence, whether she could cook or not. Her expectation of a warm welcome based on humble gratitude was definitely not going to be met.

On one particular issue they came to a grinding halt. There were a 'couple of chores', which Mrs Atworth insisted 'Cook' had always been responsible for. When Iris asked questions around what this entailed, she got the distinct impression that cooking was the least important thing in this particular job description. Iris absolutely refused to collect the laundry or do the housekeeping shopping. Mrs Atworth skewed her jaw and said, "Well, I've had a lot of loaded guns go off in my time, and you girl, are a loaded gun. You wile your way into this respectable establishment and then you have the audacity to not even do what the job entails. If you don't do the chores, what on earth are we paying you for?" she said impatiently.

It dawned on Iris that this lady really had no idea she had conceded to do this whole thing as a favour to Stan. Spending her entire week shopping and running errands, and attending to all these other nominated chores for the hostel, didn't sound like the thin edge of the wedge. It was definitely a ten-pound block jammed solidly into her holiday. She had not the slightest intention of being a general dog's body and house-hold servant to fit this woman's out-dated notions of landed gentry. This was a puny, insignificant, little farm in the backend of England for goodness sake! Stan had only wanted a cook for breakfast and dinner four days a week, and that had not even included table or kitchen duties! Which, by the way, she had done this morning because no one turned up to help. But what if this wasn't a settling-in period like she assumed? What if they never had any intention of hiring someone one else and this was it? What else would be added to her list of 'general chores', because they were too high and mighty... or too stingy, to employ someone else?

The tension between them twisted into an angry knot as they stared at each other over the table. At home in Gumleigh, there is a general understanding which the old-timers call "fair dinkum". It was about being plain-and-simple, straight down the line, authentic, honest and up-front. It could be civil, but even if it wasn't, then that was okay too. The main value was being truly genuine, with no hidden agendas. 'Real' was the higher order. The approach of 'nice and polite' was scorned. Superficial social courtesies were allocated a fair smattering of suspicion. Holding back and filtering her opinion was something she never thought necessary. Actually, she put it right up there with being double-faced and devious. She grew up with confrontation along with vegemite on her toast for breakfast, and beef steak on the barbeque for dinner. Her mother had spent a lifetime coaching Iris on verbal 'filtering' as an appropriate social skill, and a necessary expression of being kind. Maybe she was more like her dad than she was willing to acknowledge.

Iris stared at Mrs Atworth, and was relieved that she didn't have any social position to protect here. She realised actually Mrs Atworth didn't have any qualms about neglecting "nice" or "polite" either, for all of her hoity-toity Pommy English ways. Well... what's good for the goose is good for the gander.

"Hmmm. What are you paying me for? Well, let me see if I can clear that up for you. I am... or was... here to have a holiday. Stan roped me in to cook for you. And that's all I agreed to. I'm not here to run your errands or make your beds, or do your laundry. I'm not here to buy your toilet paper or wipe your bum. I cook. And I'll throw in the kitchen duties. But that's it. If that is unsatisfactory, please don't feel bad. I really am okay with you finding someone else. I'm not overly invested in working my guts out for you while I'm on *my* holiday. I'll be more than happy to go back to being a lay-about tourist... which was the only thing on my itinerary when I arrived! I was only doing this as a favour to Stan, to get you out of a bit of a spot. But right now, let me assure you that all my favours have dried up."

Mrs Atworth blinked, and the line of her mouth went even grimmer. She didn't appreciate some fly-by-night tourist diagnosing her situation so crassly as a "bit of a spot"; nor the suggestion that her establishment required charity in such a common way. What would this young hussy really understand about being 'in a bit of a 'spot' anyway? She would have no idea. She cleared her throat. "I see."

Iris was impatient. "No, I don't think you see at all! I didn't *want* the job. Stan talked me into it. But you seem to think I have an agenda here, or that it is some sort of privilege for me to be doing the chores *for* your tourist-boarders, instead of being one. So nice knowing you. I'll be going tomorrow. I'm out. Goodbye."

"You owe us for your room."

"No I don't. Stan agreed to an exchange. Cooking made us square."

"I hardly think that two meals remotely covers the cost of two days lodging."

"Stan said it did."

"Finish to the week's end and then I'll call it square."

"Fine!" Iris walked out and slammed the door. Goodness me! Who would have ever thought that the smooth Stanbury would have a mother who was so abrasive? Were all parents out to make life a misery? Just like Dad.   Iris kept walking, stomping through the cobblestone courtyard and out into the farm.   Just by getting outside, she felt the steam dissipating. The grass under her shoes padded her tread; dampening; softening; checking. She took a deep breath and looked around. Faulkner Farm was, without a doubt, a pretty place. Farms were not 'pretty' at home. They were wide, and open and panoramic. She walked over a small bridge and looked at the creek tumbling over itself. Probably they called it a 'brook' here in England. Picturesque. An oak tree stood tall; its spreading canopy of leaves, hiding tiny green acorns forming sleepily in the afternoon sun. Sheep grazed contentedly in the fields. Stiles invited her to explore the paddocks, 'dales and fields', beyond the stone-walls and hedges. She climbed over a stile and walked along a narrow lane boarded by thickets bursting with flighty birds helping themselves to insects that buzzed around the flowers clustered in behind rich greens. The music of birdsong softened the atmosphere as she walked.

The whole area was a little bit Pride and Prejudice: a place of lavender, lace and old-fashioned remedies. It was unbelievably unique... and small. Everything seemed so petite. And cosy. The lane hugged her in, inviting her to stay. The paddocks... 'meadows'... were tidy, pocket-handkerchief sizes. Even her room at the farm seemed to have been shrunken by an Alice-in-Wonderland potion. Just now small was interesting, but she vaguely wondered how long it would take before *small* became less interesting, and just cramped and claustrophobic? Wide, open spaces were something that she had always taken for granted.

Just by walking around the laneways, Iris found the tension in her body unravelling, her head clearing. She finally conceded her anger was not just with Mrs Atworth. She knew that. Perhaps a place like Faulkner Farmstay could allow her to engage in a cultural experience after all. It was certainly different to home or even different to the high-paced cosmopolitan London experience she had planned. Why not both? She hadn't planned on it, but what if she could experience village-county England *as well as* the energy and lights of downtown London?

If she gave this her attention now, it might help her to sort out what she needed to do when she went home. It always came back to this. She'd have to do it sooner or later, but right now, later was definitely preferable. Her strategy was to keep herself so busy, so distracted, that she wouldn't have to consider it. Well, this job might keep her mind occupied. And Stan had promised to show her his London. A ready-made urbanised guide waiting and willing and wanting to share his London with her sounded providential. That was very tempting. The distraction of London was luring her. But if she had allowed herself to be honest in this moment, she would have had to acknowledge London was just another way she could hide in more fog... smog. But why spoil her holiday? That was the point – to get away. And even if everything was still there, waiting for her whenever she stopped and paused, she could have a fantastic adventure in the meantime. So, if Stan Atworth and his mother could come to some sort of agreement about her being here, would she stay on? She looked down the laneway and realised she needed to know which path to take. Perhaps that was what she needed, even more than a holiday. Space to clear the fog and find direction. Still, just to forget for a moment, that was a relief.

⁂

Iris turned the corner and jolted. There was Stanbury striding along the lane towards her. Iris caught her breath. Oh yes, very Pride and Prejudice. This was a genuine Darcy moment. How strange... after everything that happened at home. Was this the answer? Had Providence inadvertently redirected her to Brightdale? She checked herself and thought about the grim, sour Mrs Atworth. Who would have thought that even the athletic, good-looking Stan had a controlling Lady Catherine de Bourgh in his life? His mother was exactly how Iris imagined Mr Darcy's aunt to be: a self-important woman who had held exacting ideas about entitlement, convention and what was proper. Iris smiled: Elizabeth Bennet had always held onto her dignity and independence, even when confronted with over-bearing personalities and intimidating conversations. Energetic, firm, unpretentious, assertive: it was a bearing worth aspiring to. Perhaps that's what Mum had meant when she talked about filtering, without being wishy-washy.

Stanbury strode to her side. "Iris... so glad I caught up with you! Are you alright?"

She turned towards the energy in his eyes. It contrasted with the disgust that silently smouldered in his mother's expression. "I am." She was slightly amazed how 'alright' she really was. Nice that he had come to check on her.

"Mother told me you have decided to go. I was distressed that you felt so poorly used. I want you to be confident of your treatment in our household."

Iris's cheeks flushed. He said *household*, not employment. "I am confident of you. Your mother, well... less so."

"Oh, that is just her way. She gives people the third degree."

"That is just her way? Oh please!" Iris was astounded. Regardless of her son's loyalty to his mother, she was the one who felt the slash of her tongue. Why do people justify bad behaviour because they don't intend to be cruel... or just make no effort to be kind? Ahh... was that the wisdom of her Mum coming back to haunt her again? Had she been kind?

"Mother is concerned that we might get lumbered with another Vino. We don't need that. But we do need you though. I need you. Please stay, beautiful Iris with the magic spatula. Please?"

Iris grimace. She had done them a favour, and yet Mrs Atworth was determined to accuse her of having compromised motives. She had no agenda! It was not outrageous to expect to be resourced to do her job as well as she could. It was obviously just Stan's idea that she stay on as their cook. As luring as that might be, she needed a holiday more than she needed his flattery. "You know, I think I'll just get on with my holiday. It doesn't seem like you and your mother have come to any agreement about this at all." If this wasn't the path to clear her head and her heart... she could go up the road... or go to London, walk through shopping arcades, visit galleries, and sleep in another clean Whitedale Lodge. Same idea, different location.

"Oh, but that's just it. We have! This is what I wanted to talk to you about. It seems you are a straight shooter, so I certainly don't want to pretend there is a rose tint to these glasses. Not at all. But we have agreed that you are the best cook we have had after a whole string of Vinos. We talked about it. We really do want you to stay. The extra jobs Mother was talking about, we'll get someone else to do that. We already have Galena, the maid who comes and attends to the basic household cleaning... and the rooms. Don't worry about it. All we want you to do is cook. Will you stay? *I* want you to stay. Please say you will."

Seriously – a maid?   Iris looked at him standing there confidently returning her gaze without any hint that he thought there was any impropriety in what he had said. There really was a class hierarchy here that felt very last century. At home she lived and breathed and fought for the Australian everyone-is-equal ethic.   This little encounter was suspended in a corridor locked in a time warp. Iris could almost believe this laneway enclosed by hedgerows became a passageway to time-travel.

She had no doubt that Stan had already assumed she was in. Why wouldn't she be? It seemed his mother was not a good enough reason to go away just at the moment... not when Stanbury, with his clear blue eyes, wind-blown fair hair and the firm twist to his mouth was begging her to stay. *He* wanted her to stay. That was more enticing than the invitation itself. "Well..."

"Cool! Very cool!" He looked deep into her eyes until she turned away and blushed. "This, little Rip van Winkle... this is very good news!" he said rich with meaning.

෯ඏⓈⓈ෨ඏ

To prove his sincerity, Stan insisted on taking Iris on the Brightdale tour immediately, showing her all the local landmarks, even some off-the-map places. When they came back to the village, they ate a late lunch at the White Hart pub, which the bus driver had enthusiastically endorsed as a pumping pub. The patrons had gradually dispersed, and Iris and Stan sat a little longer with their drinks. Iris was laughing over Stan's quick opinions and hilarious quips, watched by an antlered stag staring down at them from a shield on the wall.

Stan looked across the booth and shook his head with a laugh. "This day has been incredible! I'm looking forward to working with you... getting to know you Iris. I feel like I do already. It'll be great. Even when I go back to Cambridge for the Michaelmas term, I'll be home on the weekends."

She looked at the enthusiasm in his eyes. She was totally beguiled by his laughter and the unpretentious way he had shown her his hometown. She had almost expected an English Cambridge law student to have airs or an elevated sense of importance. But Stan wasn't like that. No. She thought about the greasy predator at the airport, and there was a huge contrast to Stan sitting across from her sipping his soda, telling some crack-up story from his college experiences. She laughed again. It was wonderful to have met such a good friend. In that moment she couldn't have been happier. She had a job she could do blind; a different place to experience on the other side of the world; a new friend. This was exactly what she needed. This was more than a distraction. This was that new path... a new direction. She thanked her lucky stars that the lady with the thick cockney accent couldn't understand her either, and sent her on the bus to Brightdale... instead of some dubiously clean Lodge around the corner.

પ્ર૭૯૪

4.

Iris flipped the eggs in the pan, swapped the bacon, stirred the porridge and turned the toast. It was like a dance for her... and she hummed a tune as she worked. Everything moved in perfect synchronisation. The Atworth's did find a general hand... but he moved on to his next adventure. They were on about their third hire now. But she didn't mind. No, that was not her circus, not her monkeys. She didn't mind, unless of course they tried to shuffle those chores over into her little corner again. She just had to focus on cooking.

During the week she'd bask in the glow of her weekend, and then just as it started to fade, another weekend would shine brightly on her calendar. Then Stan would be there, witty and charming, showing her the most spectacular scenery she had ever encountered. She had heard of the famous Lakes District through her favourite authors, but that did not prepare her for the reality of experiencing it. No surprise Wordsworth was so verbose about espousing its virtues. Little wonder Ruskin was able to say about his childhood home: *"That country is the richest which nourishes the greatest number of noble and happy human beings."* That was it. She was in a place that nurtured noble, happy people. Well, Mrs Atworth aside. They laughed their way around every glade, every lake, every 'vale and hill'. Stan would take his guitar and strum trending folksongs, in keeping with the quintessential English melody. Iris was falling in love. Not just with this new world that was intoxicatingly beautiful, but with Stan. She had stepped off a bus exhausted and fallen straight into a dream.

She hummed the tune from one of Stan's songs and lined up the serving dishes ready for the breakfast rush. Her face was flushed, and her eyes sparkled as the first of the sleepy-eyed holidaymakers lined up.

"Morning Juan. Aldrik – how are you this morning? Marie-Claire, did you sleep okay last night? A bit better, that's good. Bessie? Good morning. Yes, toast is over here..."

It didn't bother her anymore that she was not in that line being offered a warm, comforting breakfast that someone else had cooked for her. It was natural for Iris to be serving. It was a way of life for her... ever since she could remember. "Alvie... hello." She nodded and added more eggs to the pan. "Claudine..." It was funny. Remembering names came as naturally to Iris as knowing how to achieve the exact crispness of bacon that was the perfect accompaniment for breakfast. "Shamus... good morning. Dave, how are you? Dave? Oh my goodness, Dave! Dave!! What on earth are you doing here?"

"Morning, Iris," he said simply, as he helped himself to a serve of bacon. "Having breakfast, I believe," he said with an easy smile, touching the rim of his comfortable Akubra hat respectfully and picking up his utensils from the line.

She shook her head in disbelief. "You're here? You can't be here!" she hissed. He looked at her curiously. She sounded irate. This was not quite the welcome he had imagined.

"Reckon I am."

"But why? I'm in England!"

"Well, England is a great holiday destination for someone who hasn't been too far from home. Thought I'd check it out."

"You're here on a holiday? No way."

"Come on, Iris. We have the biggest barney; you jump on a plane to the other side of the world. Then you cancel your return. You can't seriously think I would let it stay that way."

"But how did you know? I didn't plan on being here in Brightdale..." But even as she spoke, she knew. "Mum. Mum told you..."

"Your Dad certainly didn't."

"How did you get here?" It made no sense.

"Had enough for a one way..."

"But Dave, this is *my* holiday!"

"Looks like some holiday... with you all over the kitchen in an apron."

"My holiday," she repeated. "You can't be here. I want to be here for myself. Alone."

He smirked. "Well, it seems I am here anyway. So, it seems we both don't get what we want. I didn't want you to leave, and yet you did. Besides, I figured a holiday would be good for me."

"One way? How are you going to get home? How long are you staying?"

"For as long as it takes..."

She refused to ask what he meant by that and turned away.

He waited, but she had busied herself cooking more toast and refused to look at him. He sighed then and said, "Guess you're not the only one who is going for the working-option then."

"Well, I'm not on a 'working-holiday'. I'm just helping out... as a favour."

"Huh. Lucky you. The only helping out I'll be doing is fund-raising for my travel fund."

"Move on, you're not the only guest here. Sims... here have some scrambled eggs." And she plonked them on the plate just a little too quickly and they splashed out over the table.

Dave stepped back and waited as Iris quickly mopped up the mess. She still refused to look at him. Finally he shrugged and sat down at one of the tables. He took off his hat and put it on the form-bench beside him. When Iris glanced over every so often, he was tucking into his breakfast and was engaged in the most relaxed conversation with the couple of French girls.

❧❀❧

5.

"Yes Ma'am," he said respectfully. He held his hat in his hands and fiddled with the band a little nervously.

"Now David, I don't want any of the usual tourist backpacker carry-on we've had up to this point. You work during the week: nine to five and if there are any call-out situations you'll have to deal with those as well. You have your weekends."

"Yes Ma'am."

"And Australian or not, I'm not negotiating with you like that tart cook we've got here either. Take it or leave it."

Dave raised his eyebrows just slightly, amused. "Tart cook? She told you she was a pastry chef? I thought she was more a farm-crew-stew sort of cook."

"Humph. She's got plenty of tart in her believe me, but my son is set on keeping her, no matter how discouraging I have been about the situation." That made him look up and he swallowed. She continued without pause. "However, we are not here to talk about Cook. Do you have any experience gardening? I am keen to re-establish my late husband's garden. He used to grow quite an extensive collection of vegetable produce."

"I'll have a look at it. Not sure I'll be able to get it prepared in time for this year. With the seasons flipped here, the opposite to home, I wouldn't expect to plant much after June. But I'll see."

"Well you know that much at least. Your room will be the one next to Cook." She handed him a key. "Here is a schedule of the daily routine. This is the list of those guests who have nominated the laundry service for personal items. It is updated daily. The service-bags need to be out for collection by the gate before nine. Everything from an exit-clean goes to the laundry service as well. The linen and towels are collected by the laundry truck and then returned at three. The replacement sets need to be put in the store next to the guest laundry so Galena can access them. The guest laundry needs to be kept clean. The rest of the chores are self-explanatory." She handed him another list of notes.

He scanned them. "Yes Ma'am."

"You can start by cleaning and mopping all the common areas. Galena only attends to the guestrooms for the daily service. Like I said, the Maintenance Room is next to the store beside the laundry. It has what you need. The maid's trolley is in there." She handed him another bunch of keys and a list of maintenance jobs that needed attention.

"Yes Ma'am." He scanned the list and didn't move.

"Well? Do you have a question?"

"Yes Ma'am." She looked up at him impatient. This interview had already gone on too long. "Who do I go to when I have a question?" he asked.

"Myself of course, or my son, Stanbury – if he is around. Anything else?"

"No Ma'am."

Dave planted his hat his head and made his way over to the laundry that was built into one of the converted stalls in the old stables. What sort of name was 'Stanbury' anyway? It was entirely possible you *could* judge a book by its cover! He was pretty sure a novel named Stan-berry would be a fairly short, stale read. He passed the other stable booth that had been closed in for the storeroom, and came to the Maintenance Room, identified by a tattered notice that was tacked to the door. He unlocked the room and stood in the doorway. The cleaner's trolley was crammed in the doorway, and the rest of the room was full of assorted tools and discarded junk: broken ladders, buckets, shovels, threadbare mops and used paint tins.

He emptied the room out; sorted the cupboard and shelves to identify what was cleaning, maintenance and gardening. He considered it a quick and dirty sort of effort, but he could get to that later. Just now he needed to know what he had to work with, and what needed to be fixed. By lunchtime he had pretty much created a sense of order and heaped up a rather large pile to be dumped. He went to the kitchen and helped himself to a sandwich. He was sitting at the table when Iris walked in.

"Dave?   What are you doing here?   We only provide packed lunches for guests to prepare themselves that they take away."

"I made it myself. And I prefer to eat here."

"Exactly why do you think you get catering privileges?   You can't expect special treatment just because we know each other."

"I'm not expecting privileges: I'm staff. Lunch is included."

"Oh? You're staff. What happened to Miles?"

"Don't know any Miles. Guess he left."

"Dave, please tell me you didn't hire yourself at this farmstay."

"Well, I did."

"You didn't!"

"Pretty sure I would know if I did."

"Oh Dave. This is so wrong! You can't just turn up here and invade my holiday. I said we would talk about it when I got back."

"Well I saved your time, and my worry. Besides, this is me just having a holiday. They were hiring, so I got lucky. Convenient coincidence all 'round."

"This is no coincidence and you know it."

He shrugged. "Huh. Perhaps you are right. Perhaps its destiny. Anyway, I'll do my job and you do yours. Should be fine."

"I doubt it." And she wiped around the bench where he was sitting. He picked up his plate, stood up to get out of her way, taking the last bite of this sandwich.

"So, Mrs Atworth said there was shopping to be done?"

"You're doing my pantry shopping?"

"Looks like it, since she was pretty definite about the fact you refused. There are all sorts of things she wants done. The responsibilities of this job are 'quite varied and diverse'. Even some kitchen clean-up. Guess that means I won't get bored, and we will be working together on and off. On the downside, it's probably going to take a while to get into the swing of things."

She took down a list from the shelf without comment and handed it to him. He looked at it with a nod. "Better get to it then." He stopped at the door and turned around. "Are you sure about the bread?

"Yes. I'm sure. That's why I wrote it down."

"I'll only be doing one pick-up mid-morning. This will need to get you through lunch and tomorrow's breakfast."

"I do realise that is the daily order. I know what I've written."

"Just checking... because I won't be running back into town if you run out."

"I won't run out!"

"Do you want to double check because..."

"Dave! I don't need you doing my job! Leave the bread order as it is."

"Fair enough."

"Huh!" As he turned to go, Iris threw the dishcloth at his retreating head. It left a soapy imprint on his collar, and he didn't even pause as he opened the door and left. She huffed and picked up the cloth where it had fallen by the doorway. As she straightened up, she saw Mrs Atworth standing by the stove watching her with narrowed eyes.

"Oh. Mrs Atworth..."

She stared hard at Iris. "Cook. I want a few words."

That can't be good. Iris swallowed and picked up the glass of water that Dave had left on the bench. She drank it without thinking. "Okay..."

"Cook. I want to make it clear that while you are employed here there are certain protocols of behaviour for employees... especially for... international staff."

She shrugged and dropped the cloth in the sink. "Dave and I know each other. He was annoying me. I wouldn't normally throw dishcloths at the guests."

"*Normally* you would not keep company with an employer's son."

"Oh." So this was about Stan. Well he is all grown-up and quite capable of making his own decisions. "Me and Stan? We are not 'keeping company'. We are just hanging out some weekends. He's showing me local places, as a local. That's all." They hadn't even managed to get to London yet.

Mrs Atworth cleared her throat. "Just as long as you understand it will never be more." She nodded and abruptly left the kitchen.

Iris sat down at the kitchen bench and realised her hands were shaking. Unbelievable! This was just like her father. Why were people so intent on telling her who can and cannot be her friends? Why did they need to control everything? Archaic! Stan, for all his trendy clothes, and modern impassioned opinions on all sorts of social and political issues, was still the son of a mother who had a highly sensitised traditional social barometer. Iris was acutely aware that in his mother's eyes she didn't... and would never... measure up. She was a commoner; foreign; *international!* That was different from home at least. At home, the Guthries were the Atworths and everyone else didn't measure up.

⁕⁕⁕

6.

Iris stepped around in her dreamy stride as she bundled her shopping tote bags onto the kitchen bench. Dave was sitting at the kitchen bench with his sandwich. "You're having lunch rather late, aren't you? It's after four," she said. Dave ate at twelve-thirty. Always. No doubt he delayed it so he would be here when she came in.

"Had lunch. This is more like Smoko. Starved."

It was exasperating that he was this ever-present shadow in her otherwise idyllic English world. They had finally had an urban weekend. Stan was on his way back to college now, but they had a particularly packed and witty weekend. She had watched him during rowing training on the river in the morning; applauded as he gave a rousing speech at a protest rally about the H-bomb. She even had time for a spot of shopping before they attended a party that evening, not exactly with royals, but with socialites who were familiar in that circle. Stan had humbly disclosed he was well known to his Cambridge fellow, the Prince (with a capital P). That idea was a bit overwhelming. She didn't want the weekend to end, and she didn't want Stan to leave when it was over.

"I've got something to show you if you have a tick," Dave said with a casual shrug.

"I'm sorry I don't really have the time. I've just come in and I have to get ready for the week. This is my what I usually do on a Sunday afternoon. And I also need to finish the menus you asked for."

"Are you sure? Won't take long."

"Of course, I'm sure Dave. I need to get things sorted so my week runs smoothly. Besides you were the one who suggested the rotating menu and shopping lists."

"But..."

"Dave, it was you who said we would not get in each other's way. Let's stick to that."

He stood to his feet, finished sculling his drink, and grabbed his sandwich and his hat. He didn't say anything, but she could tell he was frustrated with her. As he walked to the door she called out. "Dave? I really..."

He didn't pause. "You have your routine. Like we said: don't want to mess with that."

Ha! He was one to talk about routine. She stood there for a moment. Two contrasts stood tall in her mind. Stan: the entertaining storyteller, the wild adventurer, the impassioned spokesman, the bold flatterer. Dave the... huh. She couldn't even articulate who Dave was to her anymore. She was right not to just settle because he had always been there. Here she had been invited to see another large world on the other side of the planet and it was intoxicating in its possibilities. It was heady to be included in the prospects of Stan's bright future.

Iris took a deep breath and turned towards the pantry. Dave had convinced her a rotating menu would mean all the shopping lists could be prepared in advance. Then he would arrange for the standing orders to be filled ready for collection each morning. His idea was that the laborious job of shopping-lists would simply become a quick review, adjusted according to the number of guests. She sat down at the table and finalised tabulating the ingredients for her meals. It was nearly done, and she was keen to have it off her things to do. She knew Dave's system would work well. He was like that. Solid. Organised. Uncomplicated. Minimum fuss.

It was just on twilight when she gathered up her papers to take Dave her completed menu lists. She turned on the coir doormat to pull the back door closed when she froze and looked transfixed at what was before her. She sighed and leant hard against the door jam. The weedy, cobbled path near the kitchen-door was transformed into a quaint little courtyard. Garden beds boarded the path filled with pockets of her favourite herbs: oregano, sage, and thyme; chives, sweet basil and dill poked out from between the layers of mulch, tiered back towards the fence. A large stone pedestal pot replaced the island of weeds. It was planted with a rosemary shrub, boarded with clumps of silver leafed lavender standing like a silent, elegant lady presiding over this beautiful space. In the muted light of dusk, it created the ambiance of quintessential genteel England and she didn't move for a long time.

She knocked at his door. There was a pause before he opened it. Dave stood there leaning in the doorway. He didn't say anything.

Iris cleared her throat. "I... ahh... I made up the rotating menu and have written out the shopping-lists, so you have them now... ahead of time... umm.... like you asked. I'll give you adjustments needed each afternoon."

He reached out and took them. "Well. Guess I won't have to bother you for them now. That means I'll be out of your hair more... well, unless you need something specific of course. Thanks." He shrugged and went to close the door.

"Ahh. Dave? As I was coming over here, I saw the most amazing thing."

He paused and raised his brow.

"I've heard of English garden gnomes, but I never really believed in them... like the Irish leprechauns, or the Scottish wee-faeries, I guess. But there has been the most incredible transformation in that little area, near the back kitchen-door. It is a cook's dream. All my favourite herbs are just planted there. It's already Autumn... and even though all the other garden beds were left because it is so late in the year, there has been so much effort put into this one little herb garden. It's so beautiful. Stunning. Perfect. I could never have imagined such an area was possible. To have fresh herbs for my cooking... it is amazing!"

"Garden gnomes huh?"

"Well I really can't think of any other explanation, and I wondered if you had seen anything that could account for it."

"Heard gnomes were sneaky buggers... and can get a bit narky if they are not appreciated."

"Yes! See – I heard the same thing... and I want them to know that even though I wouldn't call myself a 'believer' at all... in Garden-Gnomery, I wanted them to know that I appreciate their thoughtfulness... I really do... and I wondered if you knew how I could show my appreciation. Friendly like... to the gnomes... responsible for... all of that."

"Well..."

"I sincerely mean it Dave. I need this... gnome... to know I am very grateful."

"Well, I could put some feelers out... to see if they – the gnomes – realise how much it meant to you. If you meet me at The White Hart on Tuesday for lunch, I could let you know what I find out."

"Oh. The White Hart? The pub? Like a date? I... oh... umm..."

"Okay then. Guess the gnomes are not that important after all," and he went to close the door.

"No! Yes! What I mean is... okay. I will. Yes, White Hart, Tuesday."

೧ఴఄ౫ఴ

She came in and Dave was sitting by the window at a table for two. He stood up as she approached. He took her coat and she sat down. His manner was so old fashioned, it sort of fitted with the quaint English decor. Could there be any two men more different in the entire British Commonwealth? She didn't think so.

He cleared his throat. "Do you want a drink or something... before we start talking specifically about... gnomes?"

She laughed; a soft musical tinkle. She had no idea practical Dave could be frivolous. It was kind of fun. "Sure." She watched him as he went and ordered drinks. It hardly seemed like they were childhood friends. This was weird.

"So. What was your main concern about the gnomes?" he asked as he settled back at the table with their drinks.

She was very happy to play this game. Her eyes sparkled. It felt safe. "I want them to know that I do not underestimate the effort they put into the herb garden. They must have worked hard on it all weekend and they really did a fantastic job. It is absolutely magical."

"Oh."

"Oh? What's wrong?"

"Well... there is a problem with that. I just can't deliver a message like that, although it is obviously very sincere, and just be done with it."

"You can't? Why not? I thought you said that if we had lunch it would be sorted."

"Sure... but I don't make up the rules in the Kingdom of Gnomes. They are a quirky lot."

"Quirky?"

"Their ways are often misunderstood. And they are kind of... well peculiar. But faithful. Get a good gnome on side though, he'll always have your back."

"Hmm."

"Besides... you said you were not a believer. That is a big problem right there. It is, in fact, rule number one."

"To believe in gnomes?"

"Yep."

"Am I hearing you right? You, the down-to-earth, no-nonsense, no-fuss, not-a-romantic-bone-in-your-body... this Dave... you believe in mythical little people who garden by night and turn into ornaments by day?"

"Well a gnome did turn up in your herb garden, did it not?"

"Well yes... yesterday. Right next to the sage. Red hat... blue overalls."

"There you go. You said so yourself: there is no other reasonable explanation."

"Dave, it feels rather odd sitting in an English Pub, talking with you about garden gnomes."

"Well, we can talk about what happened before you left if you like. It just seemed like didn't you want to go there."

"Not now Dave. I'm not ready."

"Do you know when you will be?"

"No not really."

"Okay then. Well. Back to gnomes. I have discovered some interesting gnome facts. Do you know what gnomes like most of all?"

"No idea." Their meals came and they ate in silence for a while. Iris looked at him focused on his food and started laughing. "You have no idea. You are scrambling for some plausible gnome trivia! Good effort to this point though."

"Really? You don't think I have this?"

"I doubt it. You work in a hardware store and roustabout on farms. What can you possibly know about English gnomes?"

He considered her for a time. "I know gnomes look at the heart of a matter... not just the surface stuff. What they want most of all is someone with sufficient care-factor to care-take what has been placed in their hands. Faulkner Farm used to care about their garden. But when old Mr Atworth died, the garden died with him. The place has a gnome-curse that will never be lifted until someone cares enough to revive their garden."

"A gnome-curse?"

"I may not be here long... but while I am, I will do what I can to show that I care. Care has powerful curse-lifting powers."

"A gnome-curse could explain Mrs Atworth's particularly grumpy outlook on life."

"Maybe. Don't be too hard on her though; she misses her husband."

"It was three years ago."

"It would take me longer than three years to get over you, Iris." It was said before he could check himself, and there was an awkward sort of pause and he quickly called a waitress over to order another round of drinks.

Iris sipped her drink and then put it down. "So... from what I can gather about the gnome, is that he will be happier... and lift the curse, if he is reassured that... that I have the care-factor."

"Not just you... but yes. Good start."

Iris leaned over the table in a conspiring whisper. "That settles it. I'm going to call him Porgy."

"Who?"

"The gnome. That jolly little chap with overalls that appeared in my garden. I will call him Porgy. It feels like a gnomey sort of name. Porgy the Gnome. In honour of old Mr Atworth of course... to show that I care."

"Mr Atworth's name was George."

"'Georgy-Porgy, puddin' and pie'. He is a kitchen-garden gnome after all. I think it is perfect."

Dave didn't blink and said most seriously. "Then I hope I get to kiss the girl, without making her cry."

∞୫ୠୡ୬∾

7.

The convertible top was down, and Stan turned up the radio. Iris took the scarf from her hair and held it up high, so it flew in the wind like a flag. It slipped from her fingers and flew through the air like an elegant egret taking wing. It was wonderful. It felt free. Stan pumped the accelerator and whooped, anticipating all the fun he had planned for the weekend. When they arrived, Stan raced up the stairs ahead of her to the apartment of a friend who was hosting the party.

"Iris, this is my best pal Ronny. Patricia needs my help in the kitchen. Quite a job being the hostess, so keep each other amused and I'll help her get sorted for the party."

"I can help," Iris quickly offered.

"No need," said Stan pulling her to the side in a conspiring whisper. "Ronny can be a real pain, so keep him out of my hair, will you? That would be a big help."

"Oh well... I guess if that is what you want."

"Sure," he said, and he disappeared into the kitchen.

Ronny stood there awkwardly for a moment and then took a deep breath. "Hey. Well, I can do one thing that Stan doesn't do so fabulously... and if we have to be honest, we both know those things are few and far between. But I can make the most amazing cocktails. If a law firm ever decides to hire a cocktail-artist, my law degree should be put to good use." He winked and said, "This is the only Bar exam I'm really interested in passing." He said it without any hint of rivalry or embarrassment for his lack of ambition in the classical world of English Law. Ronny guided Iris to the bar, cranked up the music and chatted about his repertoire of cocktail recipes, while The Beatles sang out their lyrics on the radio. He gave her a number of colourful options to choose from. He coaxed her to try his own experimental creations. He hummed along with the song *Strawberry Fields Forever* that came over the radio, while he shook and mixed and garnished with a fresh strawberry and a gaudy pink stirrer with a ladybug on top. Ronny called on Iris to give her critique on this "*Strawberry Beatles*" masterpiece, as he passed it to her with great satisfaction.

Iris was reluctant to encourage him, but he insisted she was required to offer her opinion. Besides, the show was an impressive display of creative passion and she giggled in spite of herself. "Delicious. Both The Beatles and Stan should give you an award for this little diversion," she conceded.

"Diversion? Oh no. This is not a diversion. This is the main gig. Let me show you another." And without pause, he launched into another creation he dubbed *Lime Slime*. The distinctive colour palette was definitely the defining criteria in making these concoctions. Then

Ronny made her another that was his personal response to Hendrix's song *Gypsy Eyes,* which Iris thought looked like it had been scooped from a witch's cauldron. And then there was a purple cocktail that was predominantly based on grape-juice, garnished with boysenberries and blackberries. She smiled. Dave might have said it was garnished with a fair bit of Stan-berry.

"All very 'with-it' is our Ronny," said Patricia with a wink as she wiggled around the apartment in time to the music, laying out napkins and plates strategically around the room before she disappeared back into the kitchen. Iris had watched Ronny walk in Stan's shadow on every occasion that they were together. It occurred to her that Ronny was Stan's personal Bingley, and was just as true and faithful as Darcy's friend. He reminded her of a slobbering Saint Bernard dog: big bit faithful and a little bit dim.

In hardly any time at all, the room quickly filled with college-students, anxious to let their hair down, and to allow their restraint hang loose. Stan pulled Ronny aside when Iris vacated the room for a bathroom break. "Ronny, you like Iris, right? Tonight's your chance Pal. Just keep her occupied. All night, if you get what I mean."

Ronny glanced at Stan and paused for a moment, before slapping him on the back. "All is fair in love and war then," he agreed.

"Not a problem." And from that moment Ronnie stayed riveted to Iris' side. Iris tried to shake him off, but he had become the proverbial limpet. Whenever she attempted to locate Stan in the crowd, Ronny urgently accosted her with an invitation to teach her another of his cocktail recipes... or to experiment with other curious creations. She was surprised he would offer to be so free with his recipes because she had been given the clear message that Ronny's cocktails were something akin to a sacred dark-art, with an uncrackable cypher that he would guard to his grave. This was an invitation that was hard to resist. So, she measured and shook and stirred and garnished while Ronny would stand way too close and ply her with very inane questions. He was quick to make any number of bland observations whenever her eyes wandered from the bar in front of her. After what seemed like an eternity of cocktail creating, Iris decided on a tactic to escape Stan's very faithful, but now extremely annoying, college-mate's clutches. She decided on an inquisition of her own.

"So how long have you known Stan? How often do you get together? What is this study-group you talk about? How many of you in the group? Who else here goes to study-group? How often do you pull an all-nighter? When are your exams? What are your favourite subjects? What is Stan's best subject? What's his worst subject?" And so it went on.

Ronny was well and truly bored with her captivation with Stan, his study habits and his study-buddies. But he answered every question with a cocktail mix of evasion, irritation, good nature and fake-fascination. Ronny seemed to have his heart set on making his own plans with Iris that didn't involve scholarship or anyone else's company.

Eventually Iris found a corner to curl up in, away from the prying eyes of Ronnie... and in the morning she woke up cramped and uncomfortable, her head thumping from way too many cocktail samples. She was surrounded by the contents of an over-full garbage bin spilling around her. She dragged herself to the bathroom and was sick. She splashed her face with water. Time to go home. Stan was grumpy and testy the whole trip back. She put that entire weekend encounter to down to the large quantity of drinks, a little quantity of jealousy and in the end, it was only worthwhile because of the fuller picture it created of Stan's 'other' study life.

⊷⊱⊰⊶

8.

"I hate you! I hate you!" Iris flayed at his chest; her eyelashes sprinkled with tears. There had been a weekend invasion of college visitors that had finally left in a swirl of luggage and hugs and mid-morning cocktails. The quiet left in their wake was a relief... but they had taken Stan with them.

Dave held her forearms firmly. "Ah-huh. So, you keep saying."

"I *can* hate you if I want to! You can't stop me."

"Guess so." He knew she was right. He hated that *that* was true.

"It's not fair. Why aren't you arguing with me? Do you want me to hate you?"

"Iris? What is going on?"

"You! That is what is going on."

"Oh. Well that is something. At least you are thinking about me... at least a little bit." And he poured a glass of water. "Here, have a drink."

"See that is exactly what I mean. Stan would have given me a cocktail or a beer. You give me water."

"You want a *beer*? It's ten o'clock in the morning!"

"No of course not. That's my point. Convention means nothing to Stan."

"I would argue that Stan is the embodiment of convention. He doesn't have an original idea to call his own. He's a walking English cliché."

"Well maybe, but he doesn't stick to all sorts of rules like you do. He breaks them."

"You want me to break the law?"

"No, of course not. You're twisting my words."

"I think you are twisting them, quite effectively, all by yourself, Iris. No help from me needed."

She stared at him hard, almost as if she wished he would melt under the intensity of her gaze.

"Look, Iris, it's early still. You've worked all weekend because Stan-berry insisted on bringing all of his cronies home. You deserve some time off. Why don't we grab a sandwich and get outside for lunch? Clear our heads. Found this really pretty spot. You'll like it."

"I can't. I have to get ready for dinner."

"I'll help you when we get back. Have it done in half the time. You need a break. And you can tell me all about this dilemma you've found yourself in."

Dave shouldered his backpack and walked quickly so that Iris had to make an effort to keep up. For some reason he decided that a quick work-out would do her good. He knew she would not pout or whinge; that was not her way. She would fall over before she admitted defeat. Stubborn. They slowed as they wound their way up the hill, past fields of sheep grazing, pausing every so often to take a breather.

When they finally came to the top, there was an open area in front of a clump of forest trees that grew there like a tuft of hair on an old man's head. There were the broken remains of an old stone arch and a crumbling staircase, which elegantly curved upwards, providing access to the empty space above the arch. A partial wall protected the old trees that now grew in what once could have been somebody's living room. Moss clung to the weathered stone and the fallen masonry. Someone had arranged a collection of the fallen stone blocks to make a low picnic table setting, complete with bench seats, to take advantage of the outlook.

"What is this place?" said Iris in hushed tones as she sat down on the stone table. Perhaps in some ancient past, she might have been sitting in a great hall, hosting elegant banquets with laughter and love. Iris turned and took in the view overlooking the entire valley.

Dave did not want to assume it was awe that inspired her whisper. He shrugged and sat down beside her. "Story is that this was part of an old priory that was attached to the Abbey in the valley. You can see it down there. If you draw a line directly between the two naves, it points true north... so they say. You could be sitting on their altar." Instinctively Iris jumped up and then sat down again shaking her head as she saw the twist on his mouth. "I didn't hear any stories of sacrifices though," he clarified with a chuckle.

"Monks. Not quite the picture I had of splendid feasts in romantic dining halls. That was what I was imagining..."

"Always the chef. I love that everything you do hinges around incredible food – which I also love by the way. Here is a feast I prepared earlier... just for us." He sat beside her and without apology opened up their packed lunch of corned beef sandwiches. He handed the paper packet over to her. To him this was a feast – if only Iris could see it was not just about the menu or the food. He took a bite, adjusted the rim of his hat and pointed across the valley. "I like the view. That is Faulkner Farm over there." He lent in and held her arm aligning her line of sight.

"There? Huh. The courtyard looks so small."

"Yep. Different perspective. Sometimes that helps."

They sat for a time, finished their sandwiches absorbing the panorama. Then Dave pulled the thermos from his pack and they had a cuppa, while munching on ANZAC biscuits. These were his favourite and repeated requests meant Iris kept his own private stash in the pantry. He said it reminded him of home. It also gave him unlicensed access to the pantry and a legitimate reason to bump into Iris at any time of day, while she was in her own natural habitat.

"So? Does it help?" asked Dave after a time.

"With what?"

"Perspective with your Stan-berry dilemma?"

"With *my* dilemma? No, not at all!"

"Iris... sometimes you make things complicated. It doesn't have to be."

"Dave why did you come? I had no idea you would ever consider doing something like this."

"You know why."

"But you are not respecting what I said about taking time to think about things."

"Maybe... if you were thinking. But it seems to me you are just avoiding. You're doing as much as you can to fill up all the spaces so you can't think about it. Or won't."

"You don't know that."

"I know. The way you left Iris; you were running away. And it seems to me that you still are. I reckon the only time you down tools and do any thinking about anything at all is while you are around me. Like now."

"I do plenty of thinking at other times."

"Really? I don't believe you."

"When I am with Stan... we talk about stuff... about what's important."

"About what's important to him I'd bet."

She fell silent. It was annoying that he was right.

"Tell me I'm wrong. You allow yourself to be more honest when you are with me than with anyone else."

Iris sort of grunted and looked away out over the valley. She didn't want to contradict him just to start another fight.

"Iris, I've been thinking about things too. Those things that you said... I've thought about that. Some of it was you just being mad... I get that. But some of it I've tried to take on board. Like the... well... what you said about wanting to be part of an adventure."

"I think I said you were boring."

"As I recall you also said I was staid, directionless, and stuck. You said I had to get out of my rut, and that I needed to grow." He grinned and took off his hat and ran his fingers through his hair. "See, there *are* some things that you and your father agree on."

"Okay, okay." She didn't look at him but focused on the miniature Faulkner Farm in the valley. It was kind of fitting that it looked so small. It didn't seem possible that she could fit into something so small. But the contradictory thing was that when she was with Stan, he seemed larger than life, and Dave seemed small.

Dave took another drink. "But... what I was wondering was why?"

"Why? I have no idea why you are boring."

"More like... why you said those things... and which part is really the problem? They never were before." He wasn't defensive. He was going slowly. He didn't want her running off again. He tried to lift the lid gently on the tin, so she might explore what was inside.

"I said those things because you are those things. You know it's true." And she pushed him lightly with a grin. "You are as predictable as sunrise and sunset."

"I know I'm fine with doing routine. To me it feels safe. And I want you to be safe. I *need* you to be safe. But I don't want your life with me to feel stuck and boring. I've been thinking: is there a way that we could do both? How do we do that? How do we do the adventure *and* the routine? And I thought perhaps it could be just like this. I'll find the routine; you get to experience different things... but it is based on knowing that we have each other's back. That's where safe is. If we did it like that, every part of our life together can be our next adventure."

"You're making one grand assumption there, Dave: together."

"It's not an assumption. It's an invitation. The same one I gave before you bolted."

"Dave you are my best friend... you know that. We have been friends forever. And yes, I concede you are right. I am more honest with you than anyone. Perhaps that is why we challenge each other so readily. But I feel like I've missed out on the adventure part. It's like we've skipped that bit altogether and gone straight to being one of the dull, boring couples I see around Gumleigh, who end up just tolerating each other. I want my life to be different to that."

"I just don't see how you could possibly be boring, or that being stable and sure is a bad thing."

"Dave – you are a good man. I trust you. Totally. But Stan has good qualities too. I wish... sometimes... I wish you were more like Stan... bold and exciting and modern. But when I'm with Stan I want him to be more like you. But you are you; and Stan is Stan; and it is driving me nuts."

"Thing is, if I'm more like Stan, I become... less like me. Stan might host a fair party... even if it depends entirely on your catering super-powers. But the truth is Iris... he's dangerous. He's on to the next thing as quick as anything. He never helps his mother when there is work screaming to be done at the Farm; that's got to be an indication of the man."

"He does help. He was there when Vino left them high and dry. He's the one who talked me into staying and cooking."

"Yeah see: you're doing the helping. He talks a lot and then goes away and does his thing and takes all the credit. I've never seen him lift a finger. Just saying..."

"Just saying what? That you're jealous?"

"Nothing wrong with jealous when he's constantly flirting with my fiancé."

"Dave, I'm not your fiancé. I'm not wearing your ring and I didn't say yes."

"You didn't say no and you didn't give it back. That gives me a foot in the door."

"Dave... please don't."

"Don't what?"

"Get all possessive."

"Iris, you don't know what it's like not to have stability in your life because you've always had it. I know your parents have issues... but they have stuck it out. I've seen what the other side looks like. I've seen the damage it does. I don't want that for you...or for us. If you go chasing this thing, you'll end up finding it's a mirage on a hot, dry day. It will evaporate."

"You're only saying that to pressure me. You don't know him at all."

"Every mirage promises a lot and delivers nothing. Believe me, Atworth is a mirage. I would guarantee he goes into politics after he's is bored with law. Because he will get bored... and he knows what to say to sell his vote."

"But that is not a bad thing. At least he'll be doing something with his life."

"Guess that is my point. His life. Everything is good with Stan as long as it is all about him."

"Dave? Do you want the ring back? Is that what you are saying? Would that be better?"

"I don't want it back. I want you to put it on."

"I told you: I'm not going to put it on until I know for sure."

"Well, just letting you know I'm not going to watch this forever."

"What does that mean? We are friends forever. We've always said that."

"Oh, no you don't. Don't feed me that line about 'just being friends'. I am not *just* your friend Iris. Ever."

"What do you mean by that Dave? Is that an ultimatum?"

"You know what it means."

"No I don't! Tell me what you mean."

"It means that if you choose the Stan option, and give me back that ring... I am gone. Out of your life. If that is what you want, I will respect that. But I will not stand around and 'be your friend' while you are between his sheets. Because I'm pretty sure he won't marry you."

"You don't know that."

"Pretty sure I do. Has he asked you?"

"No of course not! We've only known each other a couple of months."

"Well at least you know what my part will look like. I won't stay around to watch it. I can't."

"Dave, don't say that. It doesn't sound right; we've been friends forever."

"True. It's not right. We are meant to be forever. But from where I stand, Iris, it is now up to you."

~ೋღ☃ღೋ~

"Yes, David... what did you need?"

"Well, Mrs Atworth, it is more of an inquiry."

"Oh? About what?"

"The back stable. There is an old car in there. For its age, over-all it seems to be in pretty good condition. I had a look at it and wondered if you would mind if I had a go at fixing it up."

"Oh that. It was here when we bought the place. George was not mechanical, so I'd completely forgotten about it. But I see no point really. I have no need for a car... especially that old. And we have the Bedford for practical jobs around the place."

"True. But I thought that it might be a great little side: for guests to hire if they want to go on a picnic... or see some sights. It's a classic... a great looking car for that sort of thing. Convenient service."

"Humph. How much will that cost me?"

"Well... the spare parts and rego. Don't know what that would be at this stage, but the hire costs should recoup it in the long run. I can do a solid assessment... and then you can decide. If we go ahead, I'll give you weekly updates of course. And for my labour to get it going: just the use of the vehicle myself if no one else needs to hire it out on any particular day."

"I trust this venture will not interfere with your usual work."

"Not a chance."

"Chances? What are the chances of getting it back on the road? That has been there for years."

"Those chances are more than good, Mrs Atworth. I promise you that."

"Oh, well... I suppose you can have a look at it." She thought the whole idea was a dubious allocation of resources, even if it included his volunteered labour.

"You won't regret this, Mrs Atworth!"

Dave had been working on the vegetable garden, but as the season was running on, there was little point in doing anything more than preparing the beds for winter fallow. To be honest ever since he first saw that car, it had been taunting him. Now he had a great little project he could really sink his teeth into. He showed Iris the car.

"Isn't this past it? Do you really think you could get it going?" she asked.

He looked sideways at her and scoffed. "How long have you known me? You do know I am the proverbial jack-of-all-trades-and-master-of-none. I look after all the farm vehicles. You get pretty good at problem-solving if you've got someone breathing down your neck. People ask me all the time about spare parts at the shop and I order them in. Promise you'll come for a drive with me when I get it on the road."

She eyed the flat tires and the hay that had been stacked in, on, and around it. Dave had been progressively using that for garden mulch, clearing it away. "I don't really think it this is too much of a commitment. But if you get it going, I will certainly go for a drive with you."

"Get your driving scarf ready, Iris. Because this won't beat me."

The car now meant Iris knew exactly where to find Dave at any given moment. She knew his routine, which of course, was as predictable as a clock. Now, at any other time, she found him bent over the bonnet or laid out under the chassis. She took to bringing him ANZAC biscuits, and his sandwich with a coffee thermos so that she could she could talk to him while he had a break. She was bored with Stan away in full swing of his study semester. She hadn't realised that she would miss that part of the day where Dave sat at the kitchen bench, ate his lunch, crunched his apple, and gave an overview of what the visitors were doing around their ridges, and where they were headed off to next. It seeded Iris with ideas of what she and Stan might do when they had their next a weekend together.

Dave finished clearing out the stable. He mulched the last of the hay over the garden beds, and gave Mrs Atworth the report that come spring, they would be perfect for planting.   He was annoyed by the thoughtlessness that inspired some idiot to pile hay inside that stable booth with no regards to the motorcar. The rather loose tarp, that had been haphazardly thrown over it, did nothing to deter the happy invasion of mice... probably a hundred generations of happy mice. The damage to the upholstery was completely unnecessary in his book.

It was about then that Dave decided that any self-respecting farm-stay needed a farm cat. Again he asked Mrs Atworth, who was a little taken aback at first, but then conceded that her late husband George, and his allergies, no longer needed to dictate the pest-control program in the worker's quarter, as long as it didn't cost her anything and as long as it stayed away from the main house. So with a few strategic enquiries at the grocer, Dave came back with a young mottled tortoiseshell cat that quickly proved to be a very adept mouser and became quite attached to Dave, following him around like a dog as he worked.

Iris included a pitcher of milk in the basket when she packed Dave's lunch. She shook her head as she poured the milk into the cat-dish. "How is it, that you now you have a cat? I don't know how you do it. You could ask Mrs Atworth for a trip to the moon and she would pay for your ticket. I ask for new tea-towels and it is like I don't just want to *travel* to the moon, she thinks I want to buy it."

"All that talk about putting man on the moon is a weird thought. How cool would that be? Being up there. You know, Mrs Atworth is quite reasonable when knows what she's in for. When she understands what the pay-off is, and what she will get out of it, I've had no issues. Perhaps I might hit her up for my next trip... to the moon, and get her to sponsor my pass with NASA, so I can have my own moon-walk." He grinned at her. "Want to come? That would be an adventure."

⁂

10.

Stan came into the kitchen and sidled up behind Iris. He slipped his hands over her eyes. She pulled them away, turned around and squealed. "Stan you are here! Oh, but it's only Thursday. Is everything okay?"

"Brought some friends to visit again. We are going to blow off some steam before mid-terms start." He guided her to the window and Iris stared at a bunch of his university buddies and girls pulling up behind his low convertible, piling out of a stream of cars. They were hanging all over each other with drinks in one hand and tugging on luggage in the other.

"Hey, do you think you can pull off some good party food this weekend? I really want this lot to see what an amazing cook we have."

"They are staying for dinner?"

"Sure, that'd be great! Thanks Iris. I knew you wouldn't let me down. I didn't even need to tell them how incredible you are.... they remembered from last time how good the food was."

"Stan – the season's winding down so most of the other guests have left. I have been cutting back the orders. I didn't plan meals for another fifteen people... for a whole weekend. I need notice."

"I know... but I wanted it to be a surprise. You'll be fine. I know you'll pull it off. You do it every time I bring out some of the guys. Remember that first day you were here? Look what you did with absolutely nothing! You're not a cook; you are a wizard! You really do have a magic spatula. Vino would be proud."

How did Vino suddenly become a legitimate source of credible endorsement? But Stan had a way of making it seem totally reasonable. "Well, I suppose I could pull something together..."

"I knew it! You're the greatest, Iris. We'll have the best weekend."

"I'll need some help though. If you could..."

"Yeah sorry. I won't be able to do much – not with everyone here. Just can't bail on them. I had to do some serious talking to get them to take the break. But I'm sure you'll do fine. You're the greatest." He kissed her lightly, already smelling of cigarettes and beer. "I'd better get out there and live up to my reputation of being the most popular, fun-est host ever." She heard him hoot out a greeting and was met with cries of merriment. They jovially spread out over the common area, spilling into the courtyard with clinking drinks, loud music, singing, dancing and louder laughter, attracting the remaining guests from the Lodge like bees to a honey-pot.

But not her. She pictured him disappearing into the kitchen helping Patricia because she needed so much help as the hostess. But he was not going to miss the party to help her out. No, this didn't feel like she was the hostess... this felt like she was very firmly, and categorically, the 'help-staff'... the *maid*. Iris put her hands on the bench and tried to calm herself. Her throat started burning with humiliation. Dave. She needed to find Dave. She quickly went over to the cleaner's store and found him rummaging in the back of a cupboard.

"Dave?"

"Oh, hi Iris. What brings you over to the lowly serf-department?"

Huh. He felt it too... *serfs*. But the difference was that he didn't seem phased by the insight that his lowly position and lack of equal recognition brought. At all. "Umm... there is a bit of a situation."

He stood up and noticed the glint behind her eyes that was just a little too glassy to be delight. "Ah-huh?"

"Stan has arrived for the weekend with a bunch of his university-buddies."

"Yeah. Heard that. They are not exactly a quiet lot. And...?"

"He wants me to cook for them." She waited for him to come to her rescue and to assuage her smarting ego.

"Well. Fair enough. He's the boss."

"But I wasn't prepared for an extra fifteen or so people! All weekend! I'm supposed to get weekends off. How am I going to do this? This is so unreasonable! There may even be more coming."

"That's Stan-*berry* for you. Self-centred and unreasonable." He said it matter-of-factly and went back to unstacking paint tins, prising off lids with a screwdriver and checking what was inside.

"But... well..." She took a deep breath. "Dave I was wondering if you would help me." There. She said it.

He put the tin aside and looked kind of puzzled as he stood up again. "You want me to help Stan-*berry* take you for granted; sponge off your good nature; take advantage of your big heart and great cooking? On little or no lead-time and resources? And probably no pay. Why would I do that?"

"I know you have no time for him..."

"Huh. Insightful."

"...but... please. For me? I feel very stuck."

"Hmm. See, I have this idea that friends help each other get *un*stuck, not put you *in* a jam. Guess that is the obvious difference between me and him. So... because you are my oldest, dearest friend, guess I am here to help you unstick."

She flung her arms around him in relief. "Oh Dave. Thank you! Thank you! I owe you big time."

He swallowed and nodded and patted her back awkwardly. He wished... Instead, he asked rather huskily, "What is it that you need?"

She took a breath and tried to clear her head. Dave had a way of helping her get into that problem-solving zone. That helped. She decided to deal with this evening first and talked through options for instant party food. That mostly involved bread masquerading as various savouries; scones lavished with jam and cream; and fruit fondue sticks. Dave was assigned a quick trip to the bakery and the general store to grab fresh bread and a couple of grocery items. Just speaking it out, her ideas sounded realistic and it all became quite doable. She changed the dinner menu from quiche with salad, to quiche as finger food, and dessert was also given the small party pan treatment. As she arranged them on the serving platters, with the salad as garnish, it really did seem she had managed a loaves-and-fishes miracle. There was plenty to go around.

By the time Dave returned, dinner was done, the scones were baking; the fruit was cut, and the savoury toppings were all ready to go. She set Dave to work: de-crusting bread, slicing, buttering and cutting, while she added various versions of savoury toppings and threw them in the oven. She arranged them on trays, and then took a deep breath. She knew this was not just a culinary challenge as Stan suggested – it was a test. The test was to see whether she could fit into his set.

"Hey? I just want to change my clothes before I start serving. Can you keep an eye on the oven? I won't be a tick." She took off her apron and threw it on the rack.

Dave shrugged. He kind of thought Iris wore jeans in a particularly attractive way, so as far as he was concerned, changing would not be an improvement.

She came back and twirled. "What do you think?"

He raised his brows and eyed the length of the skirt-hem and the bold floral motifs. "Very... modern."

"I bought this gem a couple of weekends ago. I hardly ever find anything with irises as the pattern. But I had some time to explore the Carnaby Shops while Stan was at study-group. I could absolutely get lost there. It was incredible."

"Well it won't do the food any harm to be served by a pretty mannequin."

"You think I look like a model? Well thank you Dave." And with a glowing smile, a slight curtsy and the burst of confidence that his compliment offered, she scooped up the tray of savouries and took them out to the party.

Dave watched her go and murmured, "I said mannequin..." To him there was a significant difference: a mannequin was fake. But that would be a distinction too subtle for Iris in her present state of mind. She was all consumed with fitting in. He listened to the raucous cheers her arrival generated as the food was pounced upon. He shook his head slightly and loaded up the other serving platters, taking the last of the trays out of the oven and he turned it off.

As he left the kitchen, he paused briefly in the courtyard to watch the ever-present sweatshirt clad Ronny, commandeer Iris for a dance. Dave shook his head. Ronny was holding a bottle of drink in his hand, and they started jiggling away to the tune. Iris was eyeing Stan even while she was laughing and smiling with Ronny, trying not to spill her own glass. Her head turned towards Dave, but he realised she didn't see him. Dave took a deep breath, restrained every screaming fibre in his body and felt his knuckles turn white. Oh boy, every caveman instinct was demanding he dive in and drag her away by her hair. What good would it do? He was invisible. A couple brushed passed him roughly and then emerged with the remaining trays of food he had laid out. He realised then that he still held a tea-towel in his hand. He threw it inside on the kitchen bench, stormed across the courtyard and buried himself in the internal workings of the carburettor. Finally, when he surfaced, he realised he had not had any supper, but it was late, and the music still blared. His hunger turned sour in his stomach, so he went to his room and turned in without eating.

Sometime during the night, he heard the latch next door jangle loudly. He rolled over and could hear Iris laugh and giggle her way into her room. He lay awake for a while and then eventually dozed again as the guests quietened into an early morning stupor.

⁂

He woke earlier than usual and got up and went and made himself a solid breakfast of bacon and eggs. He cleared a space at the bench and ate his meal in the rubble of last night's leftovers. It suited him to get a quiet start on his day. When he finished breakfast, he snatched some garbage bins and set to clearing off bottles and picking up cigarette butts. He grabbed a wooden tray from the kitchen and piled on cups and glasses and plates and took them to the sink. Dave filled up the sink and dunked the dishes in the suds. He looked at the bubbles and thought about last night. Had his bubble finally burst? Iris saw him as her go-to person when she was stuck, which at the time was something of a relief. They worked together well; harmoniously; efficiently; creatively. He loved watching solutions materialise as she worked through those high pole-vaulting hurdles that Stan frivolously kept throwing in her way. But then he was just as quickly forgotten, lost in a world of swirling psychedelic dances and pop music. It wasn't just the drinks that were intoxicating. She was getting drunk on Stan-berry. That was the headiest cocktail of all.

He rinsed off the plates with the spray. It seemed to him that Iris was getting lost, sucked into a dangerous bottomless void. These people had an insatiable appetite for more. Enough could never be attained. For all their book learning, this Cambridge lot were a bunch of ignorant superficial phonies. He left that round of dishes to drain and went on another clean-up rotation over the courtyard with a broom. He found Ronny, the guy Iris had been dancing with, asleep under the table in the common room. Dave swept around him and didn't feel bad when he came back and sloshed his face with the mop. Ronny grunted, rolled over, rubbed his nose and continued to snore.

Dave made himself a cup of tea, and afterwards went out to feed the chooks with the scraps he had accumulated. He had revived the hen house and convinced Mrs Atworth that live chickens and fresh eggs fed into the farm-stay concept. A farm without farm animals was too much of an oxymoron for him. Truth be known, the chooks and the cat and the vege-garden were as much for his own sanity, as Mrs Atworth's good pleasure. He was missing home more than he would ever admit. He was here on a mission, but it seemed that last night had put some serious holes in his idea of what that outcome might be. Perhaps he just needed to admit Iris had really left. Of every argument that they had, it seemed that she was firmly winning this one. He wondered how long he would give it before he pulled the pin and returned home. He didn't like losing and he didn't want to admit it might end this way. Up until this point he had never considered that could even be a possibility. But he had not factored Stanbury Atworth into his thinking. His eyes were severe, and his brow dark, as he dumped the scraps from the table into the chook pen. He watched as they scratched through the slop. How much did he feel like leftovers just now?

❧⁓⧉⁓❧

"If this is a test-drive, does that mean it is going to break down?"

"Only if it fails the test."

"Well that's not good. I've got to be back for dinner prep." Iris settled back against the seat and smiled. She was secretly pleased his pile of green junk had scrubbed up so well. The guest numbers were dwindling, so meals were less demanding now anyway.

"I've left directions with Mrs Atworth. If we aren't back by three, she'll send someone to retrieve us. That will leave us a margin to get you back in time."

"Oh. I was hoping we would be stranded and would be obliged to live off the land for a week, catching trout out of streams with our bare hands."

"You want to be stranded in the bush with me for a week? Of all your hair-brained ideas of adventure, that one actually sounds appealing."

"Or poaching through the forests like Robin Hood and Maid Marion."

"Ahh. A *life* of crime. That escalated quickly from a week in the bush."

"Well, all in service to feeding the destitute. Yet, I understand of course, that would be quite impossible.

There is no way you would ever allow a break-down to happen."

"Of course any disaster would need to involve food. I could have set it up if you had let me know."

"Ah yes, I should have thought to give notice. Dave, you always have a plan. Even being shipwrecked would involve deliveries of fish and chips, sleeping bags and tents. Spontaneity is not something you know how to do."

He grinned, and shrugged, and tapped a dial on the dash as they passed the outskirts of the village. "The motor's running rough, growling like a disgruntled old bear, but that's not so bad for something that's been in hibernation for years."

Iris laughed. "With my fondness for naming things, I feel this car needs a bear name. Yogi Bear! A happy bear with a green hat and tie."

Dave smiled and shook his head. They trailed along the winding road, through the changing autumn colours of the countryside. "Yogi? I was going for the Green Hornet. Undercover crime fighting superhero by night... like garden gnomes. Those comics are a favourite of mine."

"Fair enough. Green Hornet it is... Although..." She hesitated as they turned up a rise and the engine chugged. "It doesn't seem so invincible just now."

Dave played with the choke and a significant amount of smoke was pouring out the exhaust. He found a widening along the hedge-way by a farm gate and pulled off the road. The Green-Hornet coughed and stalled in an ungainly powerless splutter. "Well, guess that means it's back to the workshop." He turned it over and it groaned without starting.

She waited for a moment. Dave didn't move. "So. Seems like our drive was short lived," he said. "It gives me a better idea of what I need to work on. Hasn't been a waste at all." He smiled to himself. He wasn't talking about the car engine.

Iris pushed open the passenger door; it was stiff and creaked loudly. She took off her headscarf and ran her hand through her hair, frustrated. "You absolutely have no idea what you need to work on!" she exclaimed in irritation.

He frowned and came around to stand beside her. "About what? What have I missed?"

"The perfect opportunity."

"For what?"

"Oh, come on Dave! You are here on a deserted road, broken down in the most fabulous old car, surrounded by the most marvellous scenery... with the person you say you want to marry, and all you can manage is, 'Back to the workshop'?"

"Well you're the one who said you had to be sure."

"Well I sure am not getting any surer. How can I ever consider being married to you when everything is so completely plutonic all the time? It feels like I'm being asked to marry a priest... if I had any idea of what a priest would be like to marry."

"Never considered myself a priest."

"It feels like it, Dave. Don't you love me?"

"Of course I do. You know that."

"No, I don't! That's the point! Isn't this what it is all about: me being sure? We are not twelve years old anymore, wading around in mud, fishing for guppies in the dam Dave. We have grown up! You're the one who said we can't be 'just friends' but that is all I ever see!"

"What if I'm being respectful... or just shy? Does that mean I have to lose to a womaniser like Stan-berry At-worth? Don't I get a shot?"

"This is your shot Dave and you're not even taking aim! Do something!"

"Something... like...?" He tilted his head and looked into her eyes. Was she actually starting to fight *for* him and not just *with* him?

"Well, I'm pretty sure the prospect of anything remotely romantic has been slaughtered, dead and buried. You are beyond retrieving this."

"Does that mean I eat alone? I can do that... I guess." He went to the boot and prised open the stiff door... and pulled out a picnic basket. "Miss Guthrie, I would like to invite you to a picnic for two... until we are rescued by Mrs Atworth's retrieval crew."

"You brought a hamper?" She shook her head, chuckled, defeated. How could she argue with that? "But of course, you did."

"So, am I in trouble for not making a move, or having a plan?"

"Okay..." She paused and flicked him on the shoulder. "Let's have a picnic in this gorgeous English countryside. What have you got?"

"Anzac biscuits, pastries, rolls, fruit and some bottles of Coke. I pilfered this from the breakfast and morning-tea stash." He held out his hand and helped her climb over the wooden gate. They walked a short distance and spread out the rug under the arms of a beautiful shady tree.

"You don't suppose there is a big angry bull in this paddock, do you?" said Iris looking around.

"It's a sheep farm... even if it is not a proper Gumleigh sheep-station sort of farm. English fields generally host woolly ewes and bleating lambs."

She laughed. "Guess that's safe enough."

"Yeah see. You talk about adventure and taking risks, but I suspect that you are actually okay with the reassurance of a life without unnecessary catastrophes."

"Says you... who has just had a mechanical break-down. Catastrophic I would say."

"I might be taking your advice. Living on the edge of a life full of adventure, danger and peril." He smiled benignly and Iris just shook her head. Dave. Adorable Dave. He didn't have a clue about risk. There is no way he'd ever be arrested in a passionate demonstration rally, whatever the cause. Stan proudly wore a tally on his belt of those types of confrontations. He even had a photo album. Whenever Iris brought up the issue of active duty in Vietnam with Dave, he merely commented, "That really isn't my fight." No impassioned peace protests with placards. Simply 'No'. "I'll keep playing the 'conscientious objections' card sincerely, until they withdraw that option." Same result – two very different approaches. Iris just wasn't sure which approach appealed to her most.

They sat under the tree in a field sprinkled with sheep, laughing about their diverse perspectives on just about everything. It occurred to Iris that life with Dave was very much like a bubble. This was one of those bubble-moments. His beloved car-project was steaming under the bonnet, but he wasn't there in his overalls smearing grease across the rim of his hat. He had created a bubble for them... in the perfect setting of a balmy English Autumn afternoon.   Regardless of whatever disaster was going on, Dave managed to create a bubble-biosphere, serenely removed from the troubles around him. Stan's world was the exact opposite: active, angry, hilarious, fast, involved. There was not a pie that Stan didn't have his finger in where he went looking for issues. As Iris laid back on the rug and looked up into the canopy of the shady tree, she was not sure she wanted life to pass her by in a bubble.

"Stan... I mean Dave... what is it that you want?" Iris asked.

"Stan? You are thinking about *Stan*?"

"A slip... that's all. What do *you* want from life?"

"Nothing." He shrugged matter-of-factly.

"Nothing? How can you say that? How can you still be back there? Has nothing changed? You still have no ambition at all!"

"I didn't say I don't have ambition. That is entirely different. But I do know 'life' doesn't owe me, Iris. I don't need anything *from* it."

"Oh." That was unexpected. That almost sounded like he had considered this. At length.

"A wise gnome once said that he respects the care-taker of the care-factor. I want to be like that. Regardless of the situation, I want to be the bloke who cares enough to put back in... grows, cultivates, contributes. Not suck it dry. I don't want to be someone who ends up just like a bloated tick, sucking the life out of everything. So although the idea of ambition and what that looks like might be not clear for me yet, I do know what I *don't* want to be: I don't want to be the tick-guy."

"Huh." She swallowed again. Why had she assumed that quiet meant zero reflection, zero contribution? She felt awkward by his comfortable willingness to be in back-ground, stable, solid, contributing.

He looked at her and weighed his words. "You say I have no ambition, but there is one ambition that has not gone away... something I want... very much." He tilted his head, looking into her eyes, into her soul. She caught her breath and held the moment as he quietly leaned forward. "Iris, I want *you* to know I love you. I always have. The only thing that has changed is that my love has grown-up with me." He paused and leant in a little closer, and an impatient toot-toot from a car-horn out on the road broke the silence. He didn't move for a moment. "Guess that's our ride," he said quietly, his eyes searching hers.

She sat frozen for a moment, and then took a breath. "Oh. Yes. Right." She turned away and quickly stood up, busying herself packing up the picnic and rug.

Dave picked up the basket and they walked silently back to the car.

Dave shook their rescuer's hand. "Thanks Mate. I'll just have another go at it. Now it has had a chance to cool down, it might start." He turned it over, and it started without a grind or a splutter. "Huh! How about that? Can you follow us back in case it stops again? If it dies on the way home, I'll get you to take Iris straight back to farm so she's got time to prep for dinner."

Iris said nothing as he reversed out. She squinted thoughtfully in the full sun of mid-afternoon and adjusted her sunglasses. "Dave Henry, I think I just caught you out! This didn't break down. You flooded it on purpose... so we just happened to stop at that picnic spot. That impromptu picnic was not the contingency plan... it was the main plan all along."

He said nothing. He put his hand on the dash feeling for that unhealthy vibration rattling through its frame. He frowned thoughtfully, focused on that unaccountable shudder up and down his spine as he drove. "Break-downs can happen on a test-drive. Because they are a *test* drive."

"Did I pass?"

He looked across at her with a grin, her hair blowing in the wind as they chugged along. "I thought I was the one under examination."

"You surprised me Dave. That's all. It is like I am finding I hardly know who you are. I've known you forever... and yet..."

They turned into the gateway and bounced over a pothole in the driveway. He pulled up outside the stables; the car backfired, belching more smoke. "*Forever* is good when it comes to us, Iris. It really is."

"So you keep saying. Thanks for stalling the car Dave, and for the lovely afternoon picnic."

He shrugged. "Perhaps you are giving me more credit than I deserve. Cannot plan bad-luck."

"Perhaps. But I am pretty sure that you, Dave, are my lucky gnome. Thank you for a charming afternoon masquerading as a test drive." And she fled to the kitchen to start her weekly meal prep. There really was no urgency. She could do it with her eyes closed. And she almost did.

⌘

<h1 style="text-align:center">12.</h1>

Iris stood at the kitchen window looking at Dave, in his hat, jeans and boots looking like he had just come in from the paddock back home. Yet here he was, working in an English courtyard with the same comfortable easy Dave way. She smiled to herself. It had not taken Dave long to have this little Lodge running like a well-ordered ship. He couldn't help it. She thought about the way he described himself – as a person who "put back in". That was exactly how he was. She watched him moving the large laundry bags with a trolley he had made out of a couple of worn out wheelbarrows. They reminded Iris of her grandfather's photos of wool bales riding the flatbed bullock drays through Gumleigh on the way to the city wool-stores by the wharf.

Just then Stan's low red convertible zoomed through the gate and screeched to a halt in the courtyard. He jumped out and headed for the house. Iris had just taken Mrs Atworth a cup of tea to have while she was at her writing desk sorting through accounts. Dave's observation about Mrs Atworth's circumstances had made an impression on her and she was trying to make an effort to be a little supportive. Besides, she really wanted Mrs Atworth to reciprocate and be a little supportive of her; at least where Stan was concerned. Iris quickly smoothed her hair and took off her apron. She went to go into the main sitting room on the pretence of collecting the teacup but paused at the hallway door as she could hear voices raised inside. It had all the escalated tones of the Vino confrontation. Iris frowned. Was that argument not just Vino's Italian meltdown after all? Was Stan having the meltdown and Vino's culinary incompetence became the scapegoat?

Mrs Atworth spoke firmly and then a moment later Stan slammed the door and stormed out to his car parked in the courtyard. But he didn't stop to say hello; he didn't confirm their weekend plans. He had promised that they would spend this weekend together. Oh? Was he really going already? Iris watched him through the kitchen window. Stan flung himself into the driver's seat without opening the doors and reversed the convertible out with a squeal of rubber.

As he skidded through the gate, he hit that pothole filled from an overnight shower, and dirty water splashed up over Dave's trousers. Stan yelled at him to do his job properly and fill in the hole. Then he sped off down the road.

Dave stood and watched him go. It was a shame Iris only ever saw the charming and the beguiling side of Stan-berry Atworth.

Iris frowned and grabbed the tea tray and went through to her sitting room where Mrs Atworth had set up her office in the corner near the window. "Mrs Atworth? Just wondered if you are finished with your cup?" She sat sort of dazed at her desk staring at a porcelain figurine on the mantelpiece. "Mrs Atworth, are you okay?"

"Oh yes. I am finished thank you."

"Umm... Mrs Atworth? Is Stan coming back? He told me he might stay this weekend."

"No, I don't believe so. He said he had study-group. All week..."

"Oh. Well that is disappointing. I had thought..." Her eye caught an empty envelope on the desk, with a London address. That was where Ronny said study group met.

"Iris? You do know that..." Her voice sort of faded out and trembled a bit. She didn't notice that Mrs Atworth had not called her "Cook". But she did get the message, loud and clear: Mrs Atworth had not changed her mind.

"Yes. Yes, I know..." Iris collected the cup, saucer and plate quickly, and also slid the envelope onto her tray, and went back to the kitchen and stacked the dishes, washing them thoughtfully. No, it was evidently clear that Catherine de Bourgh would never approve. She finished wiping up and hung the wet tea towel over the rail, then she went to the stable where Dave was predictably hovering under the bonnet of the Green Hornet. "How's the car going?"

"Better. Pretty much buzzing like a Hornet now. You can sign up for another test drive anytime."

"Well about that... I wondered if you have plans for this weekend?"

He looked up and wiped his hands on a grease-rag. "No, not really..."

"Well. What do you think about taking me for a test drive then, like you said? But a longer one."

"Maybe..."

"Well, I wanted to meet up with some of the girls that were here for that weekend party. I thought that if you needed to try the Green Hornet out again, I wondered if you could give me a lift down there? 'Kill two birds' so to speak." She took a breath.

Dave looked at her curiously and finished the last of his coke that was sitting on a drum. It was warm and flat. "So... You want to go for a drive with me?"

"Well... yes. Yes, I do."

"... to meet up with Atworth's pompous friends?"

She nodded slowly. "U-huh." Of course, he would never come at that.

"Humph. That's interesting."

"What's interesting about that?"

"Well actually, very little. Just remembering the last time you had to deal with them. You needed my help. I remember you *begging* me for my help. And when everything was sorted, you left me high and dry. I became invisible. By the end of the evening, I didn't even exist."

"Oh Dave. It wasn't like that."

"Yeah, it was. Not feeling like I want to put myself through that again. So, I think I'll pass."

"But Dave... look, I'm sorry. Truly. I didn't realise."

"See Iris... that is the thing: you don't realise. It is like you step into some sort of vortex between planets when you're with them. They swallow you up in all of their pretension and pseudo-elitism. It's not you."

"You can just drop me off. You won't even have to meet them. I won't put you through that again. I promise."

"So, you'll protect me... but not yourself. Think that was more my point. So yes... I *could* do that, but I don't think I will."

"Wow! You are so high and mighty! You know what? You say the car is running well enough, so I will go to Mrs Atworth and hire it myself for the weekend. I will get preference over your plans because it will be her first paid hire.   So there!   Take all your self-righteous judgements, Dave Henry, and don't bother yourself!"

"Come on, Iris, pull it together. That is a stupid idea. Sure, it's running better, but you're not familiar with it. Not for such a long drive. It'd be different if you were only going around the block... but out on the motorway? This is hardly Gumleigh. It's London. Really?"

"Yes really.   It means nothing to me anyway whether you think it's stupid or not! I can manage myself!"

"And if something happened, just how would I explain all that to your mother... or father?"

"You don't have to explain anything! You are not here to babysit me."

He took a breath and sighed. "Damn it, Iris, you are so stubborn! Okay! I'll drive you. I'll drop you off and do my own thing for the day. Just meet me in the afternoon so we're not driving back in the dark."

"Can I drive?"

"Not on the motorway."

෮෴ఴൈ෴

13.

Iris navigated by rotating the map to match their route and gave very short, clipped directions. Other than that, they said very little the whole trip. Dave pulled to the curb. "This is where they do study-group? Here... down-town... at the shops? That sounds highly reasonable."

"Sarcasm doesn't suit you Dave. There's an apartment around the corner."

"So, you really don't want to be seen with me. Huh. Invisible again."

"You asked to be left out of it!"

"Or..." He smiled. "They don't even know you're coming, do they? Iris?"

"Of course they do! And it wouldn't matter if they didn't."

"Iris, they might actually be studying and not want to be interrupted." He didn't think that was likely but suddenly he had a bad feeling about this. He could see his naïve Iris taking a hit, but part of him still just wanted to be mad with her. Perhaps then she would see that this lot could not be trusted, and more to the point – that he could be. Anticipating being able to say those famous words, "I told you so," tasted so satisfying. He looked at the firm set of her jaw and shrugged. "Fair enough. I'm going over to the zoo to see those quin-lion-cubs. If you get bored, you can meet me there. Take the subway."

He drove off with just a hint of that same squealing impatience she had seen when Stan took off out the farm gate. But, as he splashed through a puddle near a pedestrian, he tipped his hat and called out an apologetic, "Sorry Mate!" And all she could think was that she wished he would lose that Aussie hat. It was so old-fashioned, so totally not European metropolitan. How it never blew off, she could not understand.

She pulled in her snappy Twiggy look-a-like handbag and checked the address on the envelope again. Iris stood for a while looking at the apartment. She recognised Stan's car. Then, as she resolutely started for the door, she pulled back as she saw Patricia, smart in her modern pants-suit and matching headband, get out of a cab. Patricia quickly used her key to open the front door to the apartment block. At least Iris had the right place, but she hadn't expected security. Suddenly she was nervous. What if Dave was right and they were too busy to take a break? The whole trip would be a waste. She waited for a while, unsure what to do. An older lady came to the door with a bag of groceries. Iris watched her struggle juggling bags and keys. Well, nothing for it. "Excuse me Ma'am, can I hold something for you?" The lady hesitated and looked her over and what she saw must have reassured her. "Well, what do you know; a nice young-one. That is a pleasant change these days," she muttered.

Iris took the brown paper bag of groceries and held the door open for her. "I'm going up; can I carry this for you?"

"Just to the first level. Not as fast as I used to be."

"It's no problem." It didn't bother Iris that it took a very long time to walk that first flight of stairs. She was determined to settle her nerves. At any rate she was inside the building. Navigating that unexpected hurdle gave her confidence that she really could handle herself. She gave the lady a cheery wave and bounded boldly up the next flights. Fourth floor. Apartment F. That made her smile: a bit of a bad omen for a study-group she thought.

She knocked on the door. There was a pause before Stan opened the door. He took a double take, closed it partially, and hissed through the crack, "What are you doing here? I thought you were the delivery service."

Iris' smile melted off her face as she stared at him in his boxers and t-shirt. "I thought I would surprise you."

A voice called from inside. "There's money in my purse for a tip if you need it."

"Thanks. That might be helpful." He went over and pulled out a wad of notes. Iris saw Patricia's jacket and a couple of other lady's items hung over the lounge with her bag. No study books. No study-buddies. Her mind could not fully comprehend what she was seeing.

"Take the money and get a cab. Just go."

"Stan, I thought..."

"Well, I don't think so. Chill! I never have. Just leave or I'll call security."

⁂

Iris stared at the closed door for moment and slowly turned and walked back down the stairs out onto the street. She found her way to a small park where some mothers were watching toddlers play on bare ground while they stood around and smoked. Iris sat down on a bench. She stared straight ahead. How could this be? *This* was study-group? How many times had she happily gone her way so he could 'study with his buddies'? Her face flushed with humiliation. It felt like her world was tipping off its axis and it would not have surprised her greatly if some cataclysmic earthquake started to cause buildings to fall over and roads to split open, and she would be swallowed by some great chasm opening up underneath her. She took a deep breath and another and another.

"Hey? Honey are you okay?" A young mum stood over her.

"I... oh... I don't feel so good." She looked up and realised she was lying on the ground.

"You just passed out. Fell over like a leaf." She helped her up and Iris sat heavily back on the park bench. The mother offered her a toddler's cup of sugary drink. "Don't worry – this is clean. I have another for my Ralphie."

Iris groaned, took the cup, screwed off the garish orange lid and gulped the sweet juice.

"Do you want a smoke?"

Iris shook her head. "No. Not really. I don't know what I want. I'll just sit here for a moment I think." She looked at the sky through the bare branches of a tree where a few last remaining brown autumn-leaves clung tenuously to fine filigree branches. That made sense to Iris. Just hanging on... hanging on until she could not hang on anymore.

Then another thought hit her, running through her mind like a freight train. Dave. He would so relish all of this. It was exactly what he said all along. Stan was not Mr Darcy; he was Wickam himself. Incorrigibly corrupt.

The mother of the toddler came back pushing her pram. "Are you sure you're okay? We're all going now."

Iris nodded. As well as could be expected. She shivered. She wasn't exactly sure how long she had been sitting there. To be honest she didn't care.

Eventually Iris stood up and wobbled a little. She didn't want to see Dave. Not now. Not like this. But she had no plan other than meeting him for her lift back to the farm. She felt disorientated and it took a while to focus enough to find the place where they had agreed to meet. She stood in the doorway of the little boutique shop as the evening shoppers became fewer and fewer into the late hour. Dave did not come.

A homeless guy wandered past and sort of hung around for a while. Iris clutched her handbag close to her side and then hurriedly asked a man in a suit carrying a briefcase the way to the bus station. She would take the next bus to Brightdale. She sat on the hard bench at the terminal and tried not to think... about anything in general, or Stan in particular. But it is hard not to think when you have nothing to do but wait.

Idiot! She had been so sure. It felt so right. How could she be wrong all this time? What had she not wanted to see?

She hadn't wanted to see that these worlds were not really compatible. She had wanted the best of adventure and excitement, and the impulsiveness of Stan overlaid in the best of Dave – his honesty and integrity and his safe-ness. Perhaps because she knew Dave, and his constancy was as sure as a sunrise, she definitely knew he would never change. Perhaps that made her believe the other was a possibility.

Except Dave had said he would never travel; and yet he got on a plane to the other side of the world.

Dave had said he had no need to work anywhere but Gumleigh; yet he got a job at an English Farmstay Lodge.

Dave was the no-fuss practical guy, yet he created a beautiful whimsical herb garden in a tiny English courtyard that very few people would ever witness... just so she could have fresh herbs at hand. And then gave the credit to English garden gnomes. He introduced her to Porgy, her delightful little gnome guardian, and invited her to dinner to talk about gnome trivia from the Kingdom of Gnomery.

Dave was the 'call-a-spade-a-spade' sort of bloke, yet he fixed an abandoned green car, named it after an invincible superhero, and then pretended it had failed so they could have a picnic... by themselves... in the stunning English countryside.

Dave took her on impromptu afternoon walks, with no more of a plan than corned beef sandwiches. And they talked honestly with each other. They always did. There was a sort of raw authenticity, especially in their arguments. Yet in all the time she had spent with Stan, they never spoke like that. Not once. He had only wanted to laugh and sing and smooch. Never deeper. Never real. It was all a lie.

Oh.

Why hadn't she seen this?

This was the first time Iris could ever remember that Dave said he would do something and be somewhere, and he hadn't followed through. Perhaps he was becoming more like Stanbury after all. Why would she encourage him to be less than himself? What sort of friend would demand that?

Oh.

Why was she willing to throw away something good, for something that was not even close to better? Why had she not ever seen that Dave wasn't just good... he was the best? And he always fought for her 'better' too. He always put in... not suck it dry. That's what he said. He did that, even for her. Especially her. He came here for her.

Oh.

Perhaps something had happened. Perhaps he was in a car accident and was hurt. Perhaps that was why he didn't show. That idea created a panic in her chest, and she started to over-breathe, again, and again, and again.

~ঃOC৪~ঙ

14.

She hobbled slowly through the gate of Falkner's Farm. Her little sling-back shoes were no good for walking and she stumbled a little on the loose stones. She noticed that Dave had already filled the pothole in the driveway with gravel. Perhaps he had not changed that much after all. That gave her hope. Dave was still Dave.

She went straight to the stables, but the Green Hornet was not there.

Damn.

She went into the house. Mrs Atworth was in the kitchen finishing her Breakfast clean-up. She looked up. "Are you going too?"

"No, I just got back. You haven't seen Dave, have you? He said he would pick me up, but he didn't show. I had to wait to get the bus. I hope nothing has happened to him."

"Well, I would say fairly confidently something has happened."

Iris went pale and felt her world spinning again. "Is he okay?" she whispered.

"No, he didn't look like he was okay at all."

"You saw him? Is he hurt?"

"Saw him. No broken bones, but he was not his usual self, that's for sure. What did you say to him?"

"Nothing! I didn't get a chance. He never came."

"He told me *he* waited for you. That *you* never showed."

"Oh no..." Iris held the bench to steady herself. She felt giddy. She hadn't eaten. "Oh, Mrs Atworth, what have I done?"

"I'd say you broke his heart."

"Do you know where he is? When will he be back?"

"He's not coming back."

"But he's got to. He can't leave. He has a job."

"And that is very inconvenient to say the least. I asked him to consider being my manager. Faulkner Farmstay has done well while he was here; he has a head for that. But now it's back to finding a general hand."

"Oh no. No!"

Mrs Atworth looked at her. "Cook, you do realise he's on the way to Heathrow?"

"The Airport? Why?"

"Going home. To Australia."

"Home? No! When? When did he go?"

"About two. He even paid a full day's car hire for Feroze to drive him to the train-station. I thought if I didn't wave the hire fee he'd baulk. But he was set. His flight is not until tomorrow morning though." She unfolded a piece of paper with the flight number on it.

"Oh, he can't! What do I do? I have no idea what to do." She felt the panic coming back in waves and tried not to over-breathe again.

"If you can get him to stay, I will give him that job."

"Yes! You're right. Can I borrow the farm truck, Mrs Atworth, please!? I will pay you the hire fee. And the ring! I need his ring!"

"No point, you'll miss the train."

"No – I'll drive straight to the airport. I have to get to the airport."

"You are in no state to drive. Get what you need. I'll drive you."

"You will? Oh, Mrs Atworth... thank you!"

She ran up the stairs and pulled out her suitcase from under her bed. She rummaged around and found a small brown paper-bag and pressed it into her purse. As she was turning to leave, she saw an envelope that had been pushed under the door. She grabbed it up and ran to the kitchen backdoor. By the time she grabbed Porgy from the garden, Mrs Atworth had the Bedford farm truck running. She jumped in. As they drove out onto the Motorway Iris asked, "Why are you doing this, Mrs Atworth? It is a great kindness."

Her mouth went grim. "Humph. So, you think I don't do kindness? I employed you, didn't I? I can look after my interests. I want my manager back and don't want to lose another cook."

"Oh. Okay." Iris looked out the window. She pressed her waistline in some small effort to supress the nausea churning. Then she opened her purse and pulled out the letter. She paused and willed herself to open it. It was short. It was to the point. He declared his love and it stated very definitely that although he was going to respect her choice, he was not going to stand by and witness her with another. She stuffed it back into her purse and squeezed her eyes shut.

They pulled out onto the motorway, and Iris watched all the other cars fly past as they chugged along. She dragged the paper bag out of her purse and opened it. Inside was a small box wrapped in silver paper. She ran her finger over the wrapping and went to untie the ribbon, but then stopped and put the box back in the bag.

"You never opened it?"

"I never could. I wanted to be sure."

"And are you?"

"Yes... but I think it may be too late. I wanted him to give it to me again. Proper like. But he might not. Not now." Tears welled in her eyes.

"I see you two together and it reminds of what I had with my George."

"You saw that?"

"The first time I saw you together you were arguing over... I don't know... the bread order, I think. No man follows a girl around the world unless there is something in it. George was a man who understood love like that."

Iris gasped and held her breath. She had not understood it either. Not really. Not until now. She clutched her gnome tighter and willed that the guardian of the Kingdom of Gnomes would not allow him to board that plane.

"So, what is the gnome about?" asked Mrs Atworth after a while.

"Dave bought it to look over the herb-garden... and me. I need to tell him I was wrong."

"Huh. I wondered. My George gave me a figurine once. A lady holding a basket of apples. He gave it to me on our first wedding anniversary. He said I was a good apple."

"That is the one your mantlepiece..."

"Cook, I do love my son, but Stanbury has had a tendency to prefer flighty relationships. In town, at home, up in the country. It is a phase that has been going on for a long time. We've had others come to work for us who Stanbury recommended... but they didn't want to work at all. When you first arrived here, I thought that you were one of those girls. I'm sorry I dumped you in with the rest of that barrel of bad apples. And I'm sorry if Stanbury gave you the wrong idea."

"I think that is on me. Not him."

"I tried to tell Dave there would be nothing between you two. But I think he thought I was referring to Stanbury's pursuit of society. But that is not it. I could see you are different to the type Stanbury normally goes for. Dave didn't understand what I was trying to say."

"You tried to tell me too. Thank you for trying, Mrs Atworth."

⁘⊱⊰⊱⊰⁘

She bundled out and ran through the terminal clutching Porgy to her chest. She quickly looked at the board and found her way through to the boarding gate. She scanned the milling passengers. "Oh God," she prayed. "This is a needle in a haystack. Please..."

"Iris? What are you doing here?" She spun around as Dave stood there in his jeans and his hat. She loved that hat. He picked up his carry on and slung it over his shoulder. "Came to make sure I get on the plane?"

"Dave! I waited for you, but you didn't come."

"Huh. Pretty sure it was me who waited two hours for you. Then all day yesterday. You didn't come back. I'm not stupid Iris."

"Nothing happened. Nothing. I came to tell you that."

"If nothing happened, you would have been there."

"I waited outside the boutique. I did. But then..." Her eyes were brimming.

"Iris, you don't have to pretend anymore. I will stay invisible. I saw Atworth's car after I dropped you off. I didn't want to believe it... but when you didn't show... it does not take a space engineer to work out why."

"It was getting dark. There was this homeless guy who was creeping me out... so I went to the bus-station. I had to wait forever for the next service."

"Well, I'm not waiting any longer. I told you I wouldn't. You made your choice."

"Yes. That's it! I have. I know for certain now. I brought the ring." She pulled the box from her handbag.

"You're giving it back?" He frowned and looked in horror at the silver wrapped box. He realised then, that really deep down, he still hoped somewhere in this that it was not actually the end; that perhaps there might have been an epiphany of love. So, that wasn't going to be the case after all. No happy ending.

She stepped back and held the box to her chest, clutched there with Porgy. "No! No, I am not giving it back! I am sure now. I want to put it on."

He went still and searched her face with a frown. "You brought the gnome?"

"Yes. Dave, I have to show him I have the care-factor too." Tears clung to her lashes. "I care Dave. I really do. I never went to study-group."

He considered her standing there, her clothes crumpled and crushed; her hair tousled and tangled. She really did look like she spent the night in a bus terminal. "This is quite the serious witness to bring along. Gnomes don't take kindly to being messed around."

"I know. I know. That's why I brought him. I wanted him to tell you that I really do care. And I have the ring. It didn't seem right to just drag it out from under my bed. I wanted you to give it to me again. I need to do it properly this time."

"Iris? What are you saying? Are you sure now?"

Her eyes spilt over. "I am. I am so sorry, Dave. I have been so wrong about everything."

He stepped in close. "Shh. You want to do this? You want to marry me?"

She nodded through her tears. "I really do."

He grinned and lifted her chin. "And you want me to ask you again? Here?" She nodded again. He gave her a hug, kissed her forehead and prized the box from her fingers. "Done and done," he whispered as he wiped her tears gently with his thumb. "I'm thinking this day just got a whole lot better."

He stepped back and ripped the ribbon and silver paper away. He got down on his knee. "Dave! What are you doing?" she whispered fiercely as she swiped her tears. Her face flushed bright as she looked around at commuters who stopped and put down their luggage to watch what was happening.

He opened the dark red velvet box and presented it to her. "Iris Guthrie, will you marry me?"

She stared at the ring, wiping at her tears again with the heel of her hand. Stunning angel drop amethysts and diamond chips sparkled in the terminal lights, forming the petals of an iris. "Oh Dave! That is so beautiful! It's so..." She couldn't take her eyes off it.

"Iris..."

"They are the colour of irises! It's perfect!"

"Iris? Answer the question. Will you marry me?"

"Huh? Oh yes. Yes of course. Oh, please get up now," she mumbled.

"Sorry... didn't hear."

"Yes, I will."

"Pardon?"

"Yes! I will marry you!"

He slid the ring on her finger. Tears. There was a sprinkling of applause and congratulations rippling through the gathering crowd.

"Guess I made her cry after all. You are witness to that Georgy Porgy; pudding and pie." He took the gnome from her hands, placed him firmly at their feet and drew her in for a kiss.

~∞)(∞~

15.

Dave drove the Green Hornet up the hill to the priory ruins. He had with him everything for his own Aussie barbeque. He moved some stones to support the iron-plate, splashed it with oil, rubbing it down with newspaper. He poked the paper under the plate and lit the fire. He threw on the lamb steaks and onions. "Not exactly trout fishing with my bare hands... but if you are looking for humble frontier... this is probably as close as I get."

Iris sat gazing at the view of the setting sun. An orange sort of haze settled over the valley. "Close enough. It is kinda nice, not having to cook. I don't care how it turns out."

"You say that now." He pulled out some slices of bread. "One bushman's plate... meat, onions, and sauce. Dinner is served. Not to your usual gourmet standard, but it has the feel of home."

Iris ate it, gnawing her way around bread and charred meat. "I think when we are married, I will stick to the cooking," Iris declared as she tossed her crusts on the fire and stuffed her used serviette into the hamper. "You, however, are responsible for hunting trout with your bare hands."

"So, living a life of crime in the spirit of Robin Hood doesn't sound so appealing now."

She shook her head with a laugh and changed the subject. "Dave? What are you going to tell Mrs Atworth? You said we were going to take some time before you made a decision about her offer. We can't leave her hanging forever."

"Depends..."

"On what?"

"On you."

"What do you mean?"

"You said you will marry me, so if you are planning on going home, I'm not going to sign up for another year at Faulkner's Farmstay."

"Does that mean you would seriously consider staying on?"

"It is a farm-*stay* after all. Mrs Atworth still needs a c She's offered me a raise with the managerial tag..."

"But I thought you'd want to go straight back. Now that we are engaged, I assumed you'd be pulling at the bit to go back home."

"So, you figured this little plan was not about us doing the adventure together, but me getting my way?"

"Well, not exactly, but sort of... sorry. Yes, I guess I did."

He stretched out on the picnic rug and looked up at the evening stars that were starting to sprinkle the Northern sky. Their unfamiliar constellations blinked at him with more evidence that he was in a different world. She lay down beside him resting her head on his shoulder. He leaned over. "Iris... will you marry me?"

She laughed and held up her left hand, admiring at her ring again. "Think I answered this question."

"I mean now; not when we get home. Now. Let's make *this* our adventure of a lifetime. We can use our time-off to see whatever we want; go all over. I want to take you to Paris for our honeymoon. Or Italy. We could cover a fair bit of territory before the start of the next season... and then we have weekends to explore."

Iris sat up abruptly. "I don't know who you are, but I want to know what you have done with my fiancé!"

"I couldn't see any point in leaving home... until you made it impossible to stay. I didn't think I could ever do anything different other than farming... until I needed to get a job for my ticket back home. Then I didn't want to go, because it meant I was leaving you behind. It made me realise that the difference is you, Iris. Everything I thought I couldn't do, or never wanted to do, all of that is possible because you make it possible."

"I think Porgy the gnome was right. He is a wise old gnome."

"I always thought it was just about farming... thought I'd die if I wasn't farming. The job at the hardware shop was just to supplement that because the casual rates are so low. Getting a job at a place called 'Faulkner Farm' made it sound sort of okay to start with, but there really is nothing slightly resembling farming here and I'm still okay with it."

"Maybe it doesn't matter *what* you are doing, as long as you have the 'Caretaker-factor'. It seems that is what makes any job tolerable for you."

"Tolerable? Iris do you think I am just tolerating you?"

"Oh no. Sometimes you are very intolerant!"

"Hmm!"

"I was feeling kinda sad... that our time here was over. It is like I am learning things about you I never knew. And things about me. Dave, if Porgy the Gnome wisely thinks it is the 'Caretaker-factor' that makes you tick, what factor do you think makes me tick?"

He looked at her with mischief in his eye. "Hmm. I think it's me."

"Huh! Vanity! Seriously, Dave, I have no idea what it is."

"Maybe that can be our next quest... finding the wisdom of Porgy for you."

The story of Mrs Atworth's mercy dash to the airport so Iris could declare her love, had the community of Brightdale buzzing. For all their village parochial ways, there was not a soul who was not thrilled that Dave had made his case, convincing Iris to stay and marry in their little hamlet. They even pulled out a rather dubious legend that suggested that those who marry alongside the priory, in the line of sight of the Abbey in the valley, would have a Divine blessing bestowed on their marriage. They added to that local folklore that The Great Compass of True North would always help the happy couple find their path home.

They stood under the arch of the Priory ruins and held hands as the minister spoke out their vows. "Do you, Iris Camilla Guthrie, take David Maxwell Henry to be your lawfully wedded husband?"

She nodded and said, "I do." Her dress was streamline and simple; a little pillbox fascinator held her veil in place. They exchanged their rings and Dave kissed his bride. The view was breathtaking, crisp in the afternoon sunlight; the air held a late autumn chill. They made sure they had photos taken under the arch; and overlooking the valley with the Abby spire in view.

After the photos were taken, they went back to Faulkner Farm where the courtyard was transformed into a wonderful wedding reception venue. The conversion of the farm style courtyard to something truly spectacular had Mrs Atworth presiding regally over the guests in a bemused state of elegance. "I cannot believe what you have done here," she whispered to Iris a number of times. Even in her wedding gown, Iris checked that the food was circulating through the assembled guests.

Once they had settled on a wedding date, Iris had been devastated that she didn't know many people; at least not enough to have a proper wedding reception. Dave quickly saw, that while some girls dream of weddings of white lace and tulle, Iris had dreamed of platters of hors d'oeuvres and fondue fountains. He started writing a list of guests that had Iris' mind spinning with creative canapés and appetisers. Dave invited Galena, the service maid, and her family; the staff from the Grocery store and post office; the laundryman and the delivery driver. Then there were people from the little community church. "They're all good mates," Dave said as the list grew. Iris was amazed by the sincere connections that her quiet Dave had made in the short time he had been here. She felt rebuked that she had hardly met anyone outside the Cambridge circle, and not one of them she could genuinely call a friend. Well, she resolved, that would not be the case anymore. Another vow she made on her wedding day was that her hospitality would not just be about food. The privilege was in being part of people's lives, not just cooking their food. She saw that now. Perhaps Porgy's wisdom was connecting with others... over food... wherever she was... for however long the opportunity presented itself.

~⚜~

Iris sat in a narrow strip of shade and looked across the cars parked on the expanse of cobblestones where centuries of Roman foot traffic had stepped around the Coliseum. A giant dwarfing their place in history. They had a wonderful time exploring, and watching, and tasting many of Italy's sensory delights. But it was the culinary experiences that had Iris' palate watering over and over. She couldn't get enough of Italian cuisine.

Dave handed her a gelato cup. "Hard to imagine that a few years ago this place was swarming with the world's greatest Olympians... and a couple of thousand years ago, with the world's greatest gladiators and political leaders. And today... we sit with equal ease."

Iris handed back her cup. "I don't feel easy; I feel queasy."

Dave looked at her. "Iris? You okay?"

"I feel terrible. I think I want to go back to our room to lie down. I hope I don't throw up..."

He took a breath. "Do you think that... you know... you might be...?"

Iris' heart did a leap! "Oh! I never thought of that! Do you think so?" she said with a glorious smile.

"You could be..." He shrugged.

"Oh Dave, that would be wonderful!" But after a couple more days of feeling like she had been staked out for a Roman execution, they cut their losses and returned home to Faulkner's Farm.

Iris was usually a comfortable traveller, but this time the plane was stuffy, and the seats were cramped. She had groaned the whole way and was sick over and over. The man behind them made loud comments and drank from the hostess bar, chain-smoking to cover his disgust in being shackled with such disruptive co-travellers. Dave winked to the lady across the aisle and whispered that they were returning from their honeymoon. She gave him the broadest grin, offered her congratulations and kept passing an eternal supply of handkerchiefs to Iris with subtle pregnancy advice on avoiding garlic... and seafood... and pickles... and definitely mustard. By the time they dragged themselves back to Faulkner's Farm Iris felt like she had been turned inside out and went straight to bed.

⁂

The doctor ushered Iris into his room and sat down at his desk, picking up a piece of paper. "You are looking much better since your last appointment. Two weeks has made a difference."

Iris clutched her handbag tightly. "Doctor? Am I pregnant? I wasn't expecting this to happen so quickly. I really do hope I am."

"I have the result here." He removed his glasses and rubbed his brow. "I'm sorry Mrs Henry. The test was negative. You are not."

"Oh..." Iris felt like someone had just run her over. "Oh."

"It looks like you picked up something in Italy. That's all it is. I'm sorry."

"Oh..." Tears filled her eyes. "Are you sure? I was beginning to hope so much..."

"I'm sorry Mrs Henry. Truly sorry."

She shook her head when Dave stood to his feet in the waiting room. She felt inexplicably sad. How could she be sad when they weren't even planning this, or even when it had never been something to start with? Dave held her and she cried into his shoulder.

☙❦❧

16.

Dave was exploring ways to raise the profile of Faulkner Farmstay to draw guests in during the off-season. Iris threw herself into these ideas. She craved distraction and this gave her something to focus on. They spoke about hosting a country style Christmas with all the traditional English Christmas trimmings. They posted away some photos and put together a brochure that offered a quaint rural get-away, complete with log fire, and country farmhouse stews, and puddings – including the Yorkshire variety, the obligatory roast turkey with vegies and Yule-log cakes.

The bookings started to filter through, and soon Iris was knee-deep in planning decorations; and menus; and family craft events; and romantic hampers; and communal cooking experiences for families; creating timelines to make this the best country Christmas ever. They spoke to the church choir about hosting carolling and brought in stashes of firewood. They decided where their guests would decorate their very own Farmstay Christmas tree in the common area. They went over their plans for the week with Mrs Atworth, featuring a special activity every day. Iris started the festivities with making and creating decorations in the afternoon, to be concluded with the evening tree-trimming with carols by the fire. Rather than attempting to host a party extravaganza for those coming through, Iris sold the idea of a homely Christmas away from home, full of all the nostalgic traditions that reminded her of that other stable experience. Dave brought in hay... and made nativity silhouettes painted with leftover paint from his storeroom, completing the scene with a rustic manger and holly trimmings.

Of all the Christmases they celebrated together... this one... their first Christmas as a married couple... held in a small English countryside Farmstay, with a dusting of snow, and an open fireplace, held pride of place in their book of memories.

≈⁓ഇയ⁓≈

"Iris... there is a letter here from your Mum. Looks like a Christmas card," said Dave. "Mrs Atworth has passed on a couple of greetings from some of the families who stayed over at Christmas time. They enjoyed what you did to make their Christmas special."

She groaned and rolled over. "I'm so tired. Read it to me. I don't want to wake up yet."

He ripped the seal on the envelope and handed over the Christmas card. He took the letter tucked inside and scanned the page with a frown. "Iris... your Dad has had a heart attack. Your Mum wants you to come home."

Then Iris did sit upright. She immediately grabbed a handkerchief, sneezed and blew her nose. The weather was constantly cold, all the more oppressive now that the guests had left, and the carolling had stopped. Iris groaned and sniffed and didn't want to admit that she craved sunshine. It was the first time she genuinely felt the pangs of homesickness. "Is he okay?"

"Your mum says he is fighting with the nurses again, so I'm guessing he is doing pretty well. She doesn't say anything about our wedding, so perhaps she hasn't got that letter yet. Maybe they crossed paths."

"Dave.... I know this is not what we planned, but if Dad is not well...and if this is not just a head-cold, and I am pregnant this time, I want to be near Mum. I'm sorry but I think we have to go home."

He nodded and passed her a washcloth. "I know Iris. I know. It's time."

Going home would be so much easier if she was actually pregnant. It had become her plan... her leverage... her hope.

∾ঞ৵ৎ

17.

"Iris!"

"Yes, Daddy. I am here. I have come home."

"Well about time. Gallivanting around the globe... that isn't proper. This generation is so unstable. No sense of roots. A man nearly dies, and it still takes nearly a year to see his daughter again." He shifted his weight in his chair and looked out over the paddocks from the sunroom.

"Daddy, you didn't have your attack a year ago. We bought our tickets to come home as soon as we heard."

He glanced around restlessly and saw Dave. "Humph. Janice, what is he doing here? I have told you Iris: you are not to see him."

"Daddy... you have never said that. Dave is my oldest and closest friend. He has always been around."

"Well, I'll say it now. You can't see him. His mother was a Hobbs."

"Second cousin only. Daddy when you didn't know about that, you were okay with our friendship. He hasn't changed into a bad person just because you found out about his family tree."

"A Hobbs is a Hobbs." He focused his entire vision on Iris. His baby. Dave disappeared from his awareness. Dave stood by the door, silently, unmoved. Perhaps this was how Iris became so skilled at blocking out and making invisible what was uncomfortable. Iris' mother came and stood beside Dave and she quietly put her hand on his forearm.

Iris sat down on the lime green pouffé at his feet. "Daddy... something happened while I was away. I need to tell you about it."

"Humph?"

"Well. Daddy. I'm ready to put down roots now. I fell in love."

"Greif Poppet! Have you no sense? You run off like a greyhound out of the shoot and fall for a Pom?" He swore and leaned back.

"Now Daddy. Don't go getting yourself in a state. He's not English. He's a local. He is a good man. A hard worker. I wish you would be open to liking him."

"Nobody... and I don't give a toss exactly who... no one will ever be good enough for you, Poppet."

"Oh Daddy. I know you mean well. But Daddy I want a family."

"You have family. You have your mother and me."

"So, you would lock me up in a tower and have me die an old maid? Daddy, that is kind of melodramatic and unreasonable." Somehow Iris could smile while stating the obvious truth. No one else could get away with that.

"It's not unreasonable to only want the best for you."

"You know what I mean, Daddy. But there is more. I got married. I didn't want to wait anymore. It was right for me." She rushed through the announcement so that she would not waver, and held up her left hand, so her rings were visible.

"You did what?" He bellowed and stood up abruptly. His heavy bulk heaved and his face flushed red. "What sort of daughter runs off to the other side of the world to get married! You have no respect! No regard for your mother! Damn it, Iris Camilla Guthrie, how could you be so foolish? I didn't raise you to be irresponsible! How dare you put your mother through this!"

His wife stepped forward. "Harold. Sit down. I knew about it. Dave told me about his hopes before he left. When you carry on like this... no wonder people don't bother to tell you things. Sit down. The doctor said you were not to strain your heart. Sit down now. Settle down."

"Woman don't tell me to settle down! Your daughter eloped! Eloped! Indecency! Are you pregnant? Is that it?"

Iris gasped and went pale. No. She wasn't. And how she wished she was. How she had hoped...

Her father didn't pause, and he grunted some more. "Does a father not have a say in his family anymore? Don't I have the right to walk my daughter down the aisle? How can she come back from God's-knows-where already married? Who the hell would she...?" He sat back and slowly turned towards Dave. He had not moved from where he stood by the door. "You!" He got up and lunged. He swore as Dave sidestepped and Harold clutched at air where Dave had stood. Harold staggered and then huffed. He grabbed his chest. Janice was at his side in an instant and tried to support his bulk. Dave and Iris quickly eased him back into his chair. He shook them both off like cobwebs. "Don't touch me you double dealing charlatans. You Hobbs' are all the same! You are not welcome in this house. Married or not! Get out! Get out!"

"Daddy! Please! I want us to be a family," Iris pleaded with tears in her eyes. "Daddy don't do this. Please."

"No man worth his salt would go behind a father's back and marry against his wishes. Don't care who or how! You have nothing. You *are* nothing! You have no property. No job worth anything. You are not worthy of my daughter! How dare you? She is a Guthrie!" His voice changed to a low menacing tone. "My grandfather came to this region and was swindled by your lot. My father was born in a shed, displaced and dispossessed because of it. We come from the very salt of the earth… working our way with an honest day's work. You Hobbs' are at it again. Guthries don't just take what is not ours to have! But a Hobbs… a Hobbs will do it every time!" "Harold. Settle down."

"I will not settle down!"

"Daddy, please! I needed to go away to clear my head. I had to work out what I wanted… not just what you wanted, or what Dave wanted."

"You have no idea what you want! You are just a child!"

"I know I want Dave in my life. I love him."

"Well congratulations, Poppet. You have him. You've made your bed and now you can sleep in it. But don't expect me to be part of it. And don't expect me to pay for your hopelessly destitute choices. Go. Both of you. Get out!"

"Daddy. Come on. That was generations ago. Dave has never done any of the things you accuse him of doing."

"Tarred with the same brush. Them Hobbs' are all same: corrupt and shady to the core. His mother was a Hobbs. Now get out of my house!"

"Daddy! Please!"

"Harold. You can't throw your own daughter out of our home."

"She's the one who left. What makes her think she can go around doing whatever she likes and expect that life does not bear consequences!"

"What about my consequences? She is my daughter!"

"Perhaps she is. You encouraged this! You know how I feel about it. Get out!"

"Mr Guthrie... may I say something?"

"No! You cannot. You are not part of this family. You don't get to have a say about anything! Get out!"

"Come on, Iris. The man has spoken. Let's go. You have heard him."

"But Daddy!"

"Iris. Now is not the time. Thank you, Mrs Guthrie. Thanks."

They walked outside and they could hear the argument continue behind them. "Oh Dave. I'm so sorry. How did we think this would ever work? We should have stayed in our little Faulkner Farmstay bubble. It was a bubble... a wonderful honeymoon bubble."

"At least you didn't say you shouldn't have married me. Faulkner Farm was great, but this is your family. It was right to come home when your mother asked us to."

"Right now, I need my Dave Bubble."

"Exactly what is a Dave Bubble?"

"It used to drive me nuts that you would somehow create a bubble wherever you go... now that is all I want. When I am with you, I feel safe and protected from the world. Thinking that I was pregnant made me realise that I want to raise my family in a way where we leave the past behind. I don't want to drag all that with me. But I am not sure we can do that here. Dad says the meanest things when he is upset."

Dave grinned. "And sometimes even when he is not."

"How can you not be mad with him? He makes me so furious!"

"That story that he tells... about your grandfather being born in a shed. I asked your Mum about that. Irvin Guthrie – your great-grandfather, when he came out here... he was conned out of his place by a Hobbs who was the owner of Gumleigh Station at the time. Guthrie took at massive hit. He had a choice to move on or get stuck in it. It took a while... but he made a choice. His choice was to use what he had to make a home. That is the example I want to follow. I see your father is always trying to prove himself. He's always defensive in case someone else might take advantage of him... even a little bit. It consumes everything and it's not healthy. I'm thinking Irvin Guthrie would tell me that this is better."

"But what about me... what do I do? Daddy is so mad at me."

"Your Dad is mad about everything just now. Living makes him mad. Breathing makes him mad. The wonder is that he took so long to have a heart attack. We can tiptoe around our lives forever, or we can choose to get on and live it. Your dad talks about choices. He has a choice here too. He was not the one who was swindled, yet he talks about it as if it were his life savings that got scammed. He has so much, but he's always trying to hit hard and low first, just in case someone might take a swipe at him. I did try to talk to him about you. He wouldn't have a bar of it. When I spoke to your Mum about going over there, she told me I could see how you felt... and that it was always your choice, but she would not stand in our way if this was what you wanted. When you took off, she told me where you were. I'm pretty sure she told me mostly to reassure herself that you were okay. I don't think she expected us to come back married. But she is alright with it."

"Doesn't solve the Dad problem."

"No. But Iris I don't think your Dad is our problem to solve. You heard him. I could be a canonised saint and I still wouldn't be good enough. I cannot spend my life trying to prove who I am to him... because that is not the point. The point is who you think I am... and that together we can build a family... with or without him as part of that process. He says we exclude him, but honestly... he excludes himself."

"Oh Dave. That makes me sad. Our kids will never be able to sit on their Granddaddy's knee... or go fishing with him... or dig in the garden with him."

"Yeah... he would never be that sort of Grandad. And my parents are so busy fighting... they don't get it either."

Suddenly Iris laughed. "We are so messed up. How is it possible to have a different sort of family?"

"Iris... we take a leaf out of Irvin Guthrie's book. He stayed strong even after so much was taken away. Your Mum says God gives her the strength to do the same thing."

"But Daddy keeps harping on the disrespect thing. He may never forgive you for not asking permission to marry me."

"Like I said – I tried. But just because he wants to accuse me of disrespect doesn't mean I have been disrespectful. If he doesn't want to meet me halfway, that is not on me. I have never once been able to have a sensible conversation with your father. But not because I haven't tried. The challenge is for me to keep trying. I am only responsible for my bit."

"Daddy would never agree with you on any of this."

He smiled. "Of course. I believe it is possible to make different choices to what people expect or demand, without being disrespectful."

"Huh. And I've been told all my life to obey my parents."

"Sure, when you are three. But honouring our parents is not about just agreeing with everything they say. That is not what respect is."

"But we will never get along unless we agree with him."

"You know, it really grinds my goat when he calls you Poppet... because all I can see is that he is trying to pull your puppet strings. So, I am so proud of you that you were able to tell him about us. And you did it respectfully. We could do everything he says... and still not be respectful of him or ourselves in the process."

"As he gets older it seems he is more set than ever about bringing up past grudges. He never told me not to go out with you. It was only at that BBQ when he found out about your mother that he got so weird about you."

"I have thought about the things your Dad says. Heard them often enough in various forms over the years. He doesn't think I can provide for you. I disagree – I know

I can. I got my job back. Now he doesn't think that I have the right sort of linage to be any good. I disagree – I think God created me with intention and wisdom – even with the family I got landed with. Your Dad doesn't think I have enough property. I actually agree with him on that. But just now... this is okay. To me it is more important that we do the adventure together... all those things that we talked about at Faulkner's Farm. I was trapped into trying to prove I have enough, to be enough, but that was the very thing that drove you away. I want us to do this together, Iris – with stuff or without stuff is not the important thing."

"Oh Dave. There is so much 'stubborn' in my family, I actually think you will fit in quite well. Because, let's be honest, you are just another version of stubborn yourself."

"You do stubborn okay yourself. Your Mum told me I am already enough inside. That's what I thought about while I was fixing up that car. I am enough. And that is true, because God says it is true, even if your Dad never sees it or never agrees with it."

"But if he never agrees with that little insight, we will never have Christmas together, or birthdays or... Sunday Dinners. He is completely serious – he won't even let us in the house."

"I'm not saying it isn't difficult. Not even saying I don't want it to be better. But we can't make him accept us. Like I said: we just need to extend the invitation and if he always says no... that is sad."

"It is our fault if we upset him."

"Iris – I know you want the world to be perfect. What we can do is sometimes just a version of that. With lots of holes in it. Come on. I've got a surprise for you." They drove out and Dave pulled up outside a rather dilapidated little stone cottage. "Your Mum has given us the keys... not that I think they work anyway. I promised your Mum I would work to fix it up if we can stay here... in lieu of paying rent. Welcome to Irvin Guthrie's cottage. We get to live here."

"Really? The old Guthrie cottage? The last tenant moved out because they said it was not fit for human habitation! You have to admit, it is so run-down it should be condemned. Dad would never spend money on it. He never thought it was suitable for a Guthrie."

"Which doesn't even make sense, given it was built by the original Guthrie. If it was alright for Irvin Guthrie... it is alright for us." Dave got out and went around to open the door for Iris.

"I'm not sure what he would think about a Hobbs and a Guthrie being married and living here though. I'm very glad the feud between Montague's and Capulet's has not ended in tragedy this time," said Iris.

"The feud ends here. I'm not going to spend time trying to pull other people down. We do it differently... we build up, and put back in. We fix up this little broken-down place... and make it nice home for us to live in. I will plant another herb garden for Porgy. I can level out the path down to the old vegie patch by the creek-flat."

"A level path..." Iris held the idea, savouring it gently.

"Irvin had his market garden down there. That's where he dug the original well. Your grandfather always had fresh produce. Fresh vegies for you to cook your incredible creations..."

"Oh! That's it! *That* is the wisdom of Porgy."

"Of course. You cook wherever you go. Hospitality is part of who you are, Iris."

"It is, yes. But not just that. What you said before: "A level path"! I like that! A path that leads me home, regardless of the stuff that happens along the way. There is peace in finding the right path to walk and sticking to it. I ran away because it just seemed too hard to work out how to make it all come together peacefully. But perhaps you, or Porgy, are right... I just have to keep walking along my path... where it leads me... past the rocks and the potholes... and cooking a good packed lunch to connect with others on the way. That is the path that has led me here. And you are here with me, helping to level out the bumps, and fill in the potholes, as I am tracking my way along that level path home."

"To our home."

"See! The way you say that... this house is already part of my Dave-Bubble."

"I want a garden here full of irises – lots of them... bordering the path to our door."

"With all its flaws and problems... this will be our level path." She leant over and kissed him. He took her hand and they walked up the path into the old Guthrie hut. They were home.

⊱ఙ౮⊰

The End

⊱ఙ౮⊰

Next up in the Guthrie's Lot Series

Guthrie's Lot #3: The Crying Tree

She sat there, looking at the contorted shapes of that twisted willow-tree again. Its limbs seemed to be waving at her; perhaps reaching out, and she felt a strange connection with its tortured posture.

In this final episode of the Guthrie's Lot series, the year is now 2010. We meet Mac who has always been an achiever – a do-er, just like her father. After the death of her mother, she finds she needs to get away, so she buys a little, run-down stone cottage in the middle of nowhere to transform into a creative studio. She is taken by the feel of the place – especially the twisted weeping willow behind the house, even though it doesn't fit in her plans anywhere.

Dan spent years growing up on the old Guthrie place, so when the new owner arrives, he is not convinced that he wants to work for this headstrong woman, who is obviously used to getting what she wants, but he feels that this is something he has to do – and only God knows why.

Can Dan and Mac work together to make her dreams into a reality? Will she transform the Old Guthrie Place, and her life, into something unique and beautiful, and what will become of *The Crying Tree?*

More Books by this Author

Stand-alone Stories

Matt's Boys of Wattle Creek

Maggie & Minotaur

Homes of Healing – 3 Part Series

#1 The Beachside Cottage

#2 Petrea Downs

#3 The Writer's Retreat

Gems of Australia – 6 Part Faith Series

#1 Sapphires of Hope

#2 Rubies of Ambition